LILY NORRI'S ENEMY

JOANNA H. MATHEWS

LILY NORRIS' ENEMY

I.

THE "QUAKER LADY."

"IF Lily Norris isn't just the most provoking child that ever lived!" said Maggie Bradford, indignantly.

"Yes, I b'lieve she just is," assented Bessie.

"Why," said Mrs. Rush, who was that day making a visit to Maggie's and Bessie's mamma, "how is this? Lily the most provoking child that ever lived! I thought Lily was one of your best friends, and that you were so fond of her."

"Yes, Aunt May, so we are," said Maggie. "We're very fond of Lily indeed; she's one of our dearly beloveds, and we like to have her with us; but for all that, she's very trying to our patience."

"Yes," sighed Bessie, "I think she's tryinger than any child we know; and yet she's hardly ever naughty,—really naughty, I mean."

"How does she try you?" asked Mrs. Rush, though she believed she could herself have answered as to the cause of complaint.

"She puts off so," said Bessie. "Aunt May, I think she's the greatest put-offer we ever saw; and sometimes it makes things so hard to bear. We try not to be provoked 'cause we love her so; but sometimes we can't help being a little. I b'lieve it troubles people as much as if she was real naughty in some way."

"Yes, procrastination is a very troublesome fault," said Mrs. Rush.

"Not a fault, is it, Aunt May?" asked Maggie. "I thought it was only a habit of Lily's."

"And Lily is a pretty good child," said Belle Powers. "She is mischievous, and makes us laugh in school sometimes; but I b'lieve that is about all the naughty things she does, and I think that is a pretty good account for one child."

"Putting off is not being naughty, is it, Aunt May?" pleaded Bessie, unwilling, even amid her vexation, to have one of her favorite playmates thus blamed.

"Well, darling," answered Mrs. Rush, "I fear that procrastination and a want of punctuality must be considered as rather serious faults. I see you are vexed and troubled now; why, I cannot tell, more than that Lily has caused it in some way; and I think that any habit which needlessly tries and irritates other people can be called nothing less than a fault, and a bad one, too. What is the matter now?"

"Why," said Bessie, "you see we are all going to the party at Miss Ashton's this afternoon, and Lily was to be here at four o'clock to go with us; and when grandmamma was going home just now, she said she would take us all around in her carriage; but Lily was not here, and we did not like to go without her, and grandmamma could not wait. But grandmamma said the carriage should come back for us, and it has; and mamma says it is twenty minutes past four, and there Lily has not come yet, and we don't know what to do, and we can't help being provoked."

"It is just good enough for her to go, and leave her to come after by herself," said Belle, with a pout.

"But you see that would not be so very polite," said Bessie; "and we have to be that even if we are pretty provoked."

"I should think people might be punctual when they're going to a party, anyway," said Maggie, impatiently. "The idea of being so wasteful of a party! I never heard of such foolishness! I should think that people who couldn't be punctual at parties, and go just as soon as they are invited, didn't deserve to go at all."

"I should think her mother would send her in time," said Mabel Walton, Belle's cousin.

"Well, I suppose she would," said Maggie; "but you know she has gone away just now, and there's no one at home to make Lily think about the time. Mrs. Norris doesn't have such a bad habit herself, and she don't like Lily to have it either. She is always talking to her about it."

"What are you going to do, Maggie?" asked Bessie, as she saw her sister take up a pencil and a bit of paper, and carry them to Mrs. Rush.

"I am going to ask Aunt May to do a sum for me," said Maggie. "Aunt May, will you please do the sum of four times twenty minutes, and tell me how much it is?"

"I do not want the paper, Maggie," said Mrs. Rush, smiling as she saw what Maggie would be at. "Four times twenty minutes are eighty minutes, or one hour and twenty minutes."

"Why do you want to know that?" asked Belle.

"I'm going to tell Lily a story when she comes, and let her take lesson by it for herself," said Maggie, rather severely; the severity being intended, however, for the delinquent Lily, and not for Belle.

"Children," said Mrs. Bradford, coming into the room just at this moment, "I do not want you to keep the carriage waiting. Since Lily is not here you must go without her. It is long after the time fixed."

"Oh yes, mamma, we know that; I should think we might," said Maggie, with a sigh of despair.

"There's the door-bell now," said Bessie, who was more patient under her afflictions than the other children. "Maybe that is Lily."

So it proved; and a moment later Lily was shown into the room, followed by her nurse. A chorus of exclamations and reproaches greeted the little new-comer; but she took them all with her usual careless good-nature, though she did look half ashamed, too. Maggie, alone, mindful of the arrow she held in reserve, had nothing to say beyond a word or two of welcome.

"Yes, just what I was saying to Miss Lily, that the young ladies would be disappointed to be kept waiting, ma'am," said the nurse, speaking to Mrs. Bradford; "and I came in to beg you'd not think it was my fault. I was at Miss Lily a half-hour before I could coax her to come and be dressed; and I knew she'd be late and vex them."

"Oh, never mind. You can go now," said Lily, carelessly. "We'll be time enough."

"Come, let us go now," said Maggie, with an expression which showed that she by no means agreed with Lily that it was "time enough;" and good-by being said to mamma and Mrs. Rush, she led the way from the room, followed by the rest of the young party, who were soon seated snugly in the carriage.

"Lily," said Maggie, as soon as they had fairly started, "I have a story to tell you about punctuality."

"Pooh! I don't want to hear about your old punctuality," said Lily. "Everybody just bothers me 'most to death about being punctual. Tom has been making a fuss about it just now."

"But it is a story,—one of Maggie's stories," said Belle, who thought it quite incredible that any one should decline an opportunity of hearing one of those interesting and valuable narratives.

"Let's hear it then," said Lily.

"It is not a story of my own making up," said Maggie, with the solemnity which befitted a teacher of moral lessons; "but it is very interesting, and may do some good, if people choose to let it. But as there are 'none so deaf as those who won't hear,' so I suppose there are none so hard to teach as those who won't be taught."

"But what is the story?" asked Belle.

"The story is this," answered Maggie. "Once thirteen ladies went to a meeting, or ought to go to a meeting. Well, twelve of them came at the right time to the house of a very wise old Quaker lady, where the meeting was; but the thirteenth lady did not come for a quarter of an hour after she ought to. So the other ladies were as tired as they could be, 'cause they couldn't begin to do what they had to do without her—but I would have if I'd been there—and some of them yawned—which wasn't polite for them to do, but they could hardly help it—and some went to sleep, and some had headaches, and one who was sitting in a breeze from the window, where she didn't like to sit, took cold, and had a sore throat and a toothache, and she had to go and have her tooth out; which was all the fault of the unpunctual lady, and I should think she'd be very much ashamed of herself."

"So should I," said Mabel, as Maggie paused to take breath.

"What's the rest of the story?" asked Bessie, impatient of delay in such a thrilling tale.

"Well, when she came in," continued Maggie, giving point to her story by the look she fixed upon Lily,—"when she came in, after doing such a lot of mischief, she didn't seem to think it was any great harm after all; but she just said, 'Ladies, I am sorry I kept you waiting, but it is only a quarter of an hour.' Then the wise old Quaker lady stood up and looked very severe at her, and she said, 'Friend, thee'— thee is the way Quakers say you—'Friend, thee has wasted three hours of time that did not belong to thee. Here are twelve of us, and a quarter of an hour for each makes three hours, and you—thee, I mean—had no right to do it, and thee ought to be ashamed of yourself.' And the lady was ashamed of herself, 'cause it made her feel horridly to be talked to that way before so many people; and she never did so again, which was a great blessing to every one who knew her, because she made herself a great inconvenience."

And here Maggie closed her story, which she had one day lately found in some book or paper, and had brought it up on this occasion for Lily's benefit, adding to it sundry embellishments of her own, which, as she thought, made it more telling and serviceable.

"But," said Lily, who took the moral to herself as it was intended she should do, "but we're not a meeting, and you're not a Quaker lady, Maggie. It's only a party."

"Only a party!" echoed Maggie, in an aggrieved tone, which told that this was adding insult to injury; "she says, 'Only a party'! Now, Lily, I don't want to hurt your feelings, but I just want to tell you something."

And Maggie held up the bit of paper on which she had taken the pains to note down the sum Mrs. Rush had done for her, lest she should forget the number of minutes.

"You kept us waiting more than twenty minutes, Lily. Miss Ashton invited us at four, and you did not come till twenty minutes after; and there are four of us besides yourself, so there's one whole hour, and forty minutes,—which is 'most three-quarters of an hour,—one whole hour and forty minutes of party wasted, and only twenty minutes of it was your own."

"And I'm sure it's a great deal harder to have a party wasted than it is a meeting," said Belle.

"I never thought about it," said Lily, by no means offended, but considerably astonished at the way in which her short-comings were brought home to her. "I never thought of that, and I'm real sorry. I'll never do it again."

"Did the lady with the toothache ever tell the late lady she made her have it?" asked Bessie.

"Well, I'm not very sure," said Maggie, not willing to confess to total ignorance on this subject; "but I think she did."

"Then she wasn't very kind," said Bessie. "It would have been kinder if she hadn't spoken about it. She had lesson enough. I think that old Quaker lady was pretty cross, and I'm glad she's not my grandmamma."

"Maggie," said Lily, as the carriage drew up at Miss Ashton's door, "couldn't you make me a proverb picture about putting off? I would like one ever so much."

For Lily took great delight in these same "proverb pictures," and was very glad to receive one even when it held up her own failings to reproof.

"Is there any proverb about putting off?" asked Belle.

"Yes, to be sure," said Lily. "There's 'Sufficient unto the day is the evil thereof.'"

"Um—I don't know," said Maggie, doubtful if this adage were quite applicable to the case in question. "I don't think that will do; but if we can't find one, we'll make one, and draw you a proverb picture about it. I'll ask mamma if she knows of any that will do."

"And make it for me very soon, will you?" said Lily, jumping from the carriage with the assistance of Mrs. Ashton's maid, who had come to take them out. "I'll try to have it do me some good."

This was encouraging, and Maggie's imagination was at once put to work; but not to much purpose for this evening, since as yet she knew of no proverb that would answer for the object she had in view.

Our young party was greeted with a chorus of welcome, not only from Mrs. and Miss Ashton, but also from the other little girls who had all arrived before them; for children are generally punctual to such engagements, whatever their elders may be. Indeed, they usually prefer to be before, rather than after the time.

"How late you came!"

"What kept you?"

"It's more than half-past four!"

"We've been here ever so long."

"We've been waiting for you"—and such like exclamations met them on all sides.

7

"It's my fault," said Lily. "I was not ready in time, and kept them waiting."

"O Lily!" said Carrie Ransom. "You always do keep people waiting."

"Well, I can't help it," said Lily.

"Yes, you can," said Gracie Howard; "at least, you could if you would do things in time; but you never will."

"I'll grow out of it when I'm bigger," said Lily. "People 'most always cure up their faults before they're grown up."

"Not if they don't take pains with them when they're little," said Bessie, solemnly. "Lily, if you keep on per-cas-ter-nating now, maybe you won't be able to help it when you're grown up, and then people will be provoked with you."

"Were you much provoked with me to-day?" asked Lily.

"Um-m, pretty," said Bessie; "but we're quite over it now."

"Well, I don't care much then," was Lily's thought; but she said aloud, "I don't think it can do much harm when we're little. You see we're all here now. But I will begin pretty soon to correct myself of it."

"She had better begin to-day," thought Bessie; but no more was said on the subject, and they were all soon engaged in a merry game of play.

The party passed off pleasantly, so pleasantly that Maggie found more and more cause for regret that she and her own particular friends had been unjustly defrauded, as she considered it, of so large a portion of it; but she was too forgiving and good-natured to reproach Lily any farther, especially as Bessie privately confided to her that she did not like "that severe old Quaker lady one bit, and am very glad that she is not one of my friends."

Maggie thought that perhaps she had been rather severe herself, and took pains to be especially agreeable to Lily for the rest of the day.

But perhaps this ready forgetfulness of their vexation was not the best thing for heedless, light-hearted Lily. At first she had felt a little self-reproachful, but when she saw the other children forget their momentary displeasure, she thought her own troublesome want of punctuality did not matter much after all; they were all glad and happy now, and some of these days she would try to break herself of this bad habit.

Ah! you see, that was Lily's way; it was always "one of these days," "some other time," "by and by;" and here lay the root of the trouble which proved so vexatious to those about her, and very often to herself.

"Mamma," said Maggie, as soon as they reached home, "do you know of any proverb that would be a good correction of the habit of putting off, and never being ready in time?"

Mrs. Bradford laughed.

"Yes, I think I do, Maggie. What do you want to do with it?"

"To make a proverb picture for Lily, mamma; she wants us to. She likes our proverb pictures very much, and never is provoked when we give her one. And I think I shall write her a piece of poetry about it too. What is the proverb, mamma?"

"I will tell you in the morning, dear."

"Why not to-night, mamma?"

"Because I want you to go to sleep now, Maggie. If I tell you a proverb to-night, you will lie awake, turning it over in your mind, and making verses and pictures for it; and I do not wish you to do that. Wait till morning, dear."

Maggie submitted, like the docile and obedient little girl she was, though she was disappointed; for as mamma knew, she would have liked to spend part of her proper sleeping time in composing verses, and inventing pictures for Lily's benefit.

"Shall you make the poetry a divine song, or a moral poem?" asked Bessie, who took the greatest possible interest and pride in Maggie's poetical attempts.

"I think I'll mix the two," said Maggie, after a little deliberation. "It might be better, because Lily don't care much to read things that are very pious; but she needs them a little. Yes, I'll do that."

And now, according to mamma's orders, they ceased talking; and Maggie, obeying not only the letter, but the spirit of her mother's command, tried to put from her all thought of the lesson she was to teach Lily, and both she and Bessie were soon fast asleep.

II.

A MONKEY, A PUPPY, AND A BEGGAR.

"LILY!"

"Yes, mamma!"

"Can I trust you to do something for me?"

"Yes, indeed, mamma! you know I like to help you."

"I want it done immediately, dear."

"Oh, yes, mamma, I'm ready. I'll do it right away."

Mrs. Norris sat at the library table, writing. As she said the last words she hastily folded the note she had just finished, and slipped it into its envelope; then, as she put the address upon it, she said, —

"I have an appointment to keep, Lily; and there is Mrs. Bradford now, I believe. I am going with her, and I would like you to lay these papers smoothly in my writing-case, those others in this box, — you know where they belong, — and to put my silver inkstand carefully in the secretary. There, I have closed it, so you cannot spill the ink. Will you be a helpful little girl, and see to that for me, my daughter?"

"Yes, indeed, mamma," said Lily again. "I'm glad you let me do it for you. I'll be very careful with the inkstand."

"And at once, remember, dear," said Mrs. Norris, rising from her chair. "I do not wish the inkstand left here on the table, or the paper to lie scattered about. It will be a great help to mamma if you do it nicely. Ah! good afternoon, Mrs. Bradford," as that lady was shown into the room. "I am all ready, and will not detain you. I had just received a note which needed an immediate answer, before I left home; but it is finished, and I shall trust Lily to put by my writing materials for me."

Lily looked up at Mrs. Bradford, rather proud of being trusted by her mother; and the lady smiled as she stooped to kiss her.

"Lily likes to help mamma as well as Maggie and Bessie do, I see," she said.

"Yes: and she can often be of great assistance when she is prompt and punctual," said Mrs. Norris, drawing on her gloves.

"Are Maggie and Bessie well, Mrs. Bradford?" asked Lily.

"Yes, dear; and they wished me to ask you to come and see them very soon. I do not know when they want you to come, for they have some plans to arrange with their Aunt Annie, but they will let you know. They are drawing some pictures for you, I believe, and want to explain it to you."

"Oh, yes," said Lily; "they promised me a proverb picture, and their proverb pictures are so interesting. I should think any one might be glad to have them."

"They certainly seem to give great satisfaction, both to themselves, and to those whom they are intended to benefit," said Mrs. Bradford, laughing. "Good-by, Lily. The children will see you soon. I gave them leave to ask you when they pleased; and you must come early, whenever that may be."

"Thank you, ma'am," said Lily. "I'll come just as soon as mamma will let me."

She followed her mother and Mrs. Bradford to the front door, where the former turned, and said a little uneasily,—

"Lily, attend to the inkstand at once, my darling."

"I am going to, mamma," answered the little girl, meaning what she said at the moment, though she afterwards came so far short of it, as you shall see.

As the door closed after the two ladies, Lily caught the notes of a hand-organ in the street; and running back to the library, she went to the window to look out for the strolling musician who carried it.

She had not forgotten her mother's orders, or the help she had promised to be to her; and as she passed by the table on her way to the window, the scattered papers and the silver inkstand caught her eye, and reminded her of her promise.

But she did not pause.

"Just a moment; I'll put them away in one moment," she said to herself. "I'll just look and see if that organ man is coming here; 'cause I have some pennies in my pocket, and I'll give him some. Oh, yes! there he is, and he has a monkey. I like monkey organ men the best, 'cause the monkeys are so funny. What a funny fellow! Why, he's 'most the cunningest monkey I ever saw;" and Lily had quite forgotten her promise.

She was in great glee over the monkey, who certainly was a droll, though a very ugly little beast, as monkeys generally are; and she amused herself with him for some time, as he climbed the balcony railings, stoop, and blinds, hopped up and down the broad stone steps, and every now and then came close to the window where she stood, and mouthed and jabbered away at her. Amused though she was, she was glad that the glass was between her and the grinning creature; and she always took the opportunity of his little excursions to open the window and quickly thrust out the pennies, for which he immediately sprang down, and taking them up in his paw hurried with them to his master. Lily treated him also to a cake, which he greedily nibbled; and then, seeing that the poor creature lapped his tongue upon a damp spot on the stone pavement, where a little water had been spilled, as though he were thirsty, she called a servant to bring a cup of water, and gave him a drink.

Finding that she thus provided entertainment for man and beast, and that he was reaping quite a harvest, the organ-grinder stayed for some time; and all the while, the inkstand remained unheeded on the table. Not quite forgotten, either; for every now and then the recollection of it would come to her; but Lily kept saying to herself, "In one minute; I'm going in just one minute."

But the one minute multiplied itself into twenty before the man moved off with his organ and his monkey, and Lily felt at leisure to attend to her mother's wishes.

But it seemed after all that the time had not yet come.

"Miss Lily," said a servant man, putting his head in at the library door, "is Master Tom at home?"

"No, I b'lieve not; I think he didn't come from school yet," answered Lily, with her hand on the inkstand.

"I'd like to know what time he'll be in," said the man, lingering, "for my brother is below with the puppies Master Tom wanted to see. There's a gentleman wants to buy both; but seeing Master Tom had spoken about one if it suited, he thought it was only fair to bring them here first, and let him make up his mind. But the gentleman must know this afternoon. Wouldn't you like to see 'em, Miss Lily? They're such pretty little dogs."

"Yes, indeed I would," answered the child; and she followed the man to the basement hall, where his brother waited with the puppies, — not without another thought of her still unperformed duty; but again she contented herself with the excuse, "I shan't be half a minute, and the inkstand is shut up. It can't spill the ink."

Alas, alas! it was long before the recollection of it again crossed Lily's mind.

If she had found the monkey bewitching, what did she find the little dogs, — playful, pretty creatures, which seemed delighted with a playmate frolicsome and mischievous as themselves?

Then her brother Tom came in; and, hearing that the dogs were there for his approval, came down to look at them and decide which he would have.

Of course Lily must stay and help him to make his choice; and now that vexatious little feeling that there was something wrong, some duty unfulfilled, had altogether passed away. Lily was quite at her ease by this time.

The matter was at last settled; the dog chosen, the man paid and sent away, leaving the selected puppy in a very low and melancholy state of mind at the parting. He whined and cried piteously, first scratching and barking at the door where his former owner and his puppy brother had passed out; and at last, after refusing to be comforted by all the petting that was lavished upon him, retiring into private life behind the kitchen coal-scuttle, and resolutely declining to be coaxed out.

"Never mind," said Tom, "he'll be all right by and by, Lily. Wait till he's hungry, and he'll come out and be glad enough to make friends. Now I am going to buy a house for him. I saw some pretty little dog-houses down at Bruner's this morning, and I'll go look at them, and see if they'll answer."

"Oh, Tom! could I go with you?" asked Lily.

"Yes, if you like," said Tom; "I'll be glad to have you; only make haste to be dressed, Lily. Will you go to Nora at once?"

"Yes, yes," said Lily, clapping her hands; and away she flew to beg her nurse to make her ready as soon as possible.

Nothing presenting itself just then to take up her attention, or which looked more attractive than the promised walk with Tom, she made no delay, but obeyed his direction to go and be dressed at once.

How many boys do you think would have consented as readily, cheerfully, and kindly as Tom Norris did to such a request from a little sister? But that was Tom's way. When he granted a favor or bestowed a kindness, it was done in a manner which made it seem as if it were a pleasure to himself. And if he were obliged to refuse Lily any thing that she asked, she never grumbled nor fretted, because she knew well that Tom would grant it if he could, or if it were best for her to have it. Tom never said he couldn't be "bothered with girls," or "catch me doing it," or ran off with some other contemptuous or unkind speech, such as boys too often use toward their little sisters. Tom was a true man, and a true gentleman, kindly and courteous in his manner and words toward all women and children, but especially to his mother and little sister: free, fearless, and generous; daring to do and to speak the right; yet so bright, so gay, so manly that not one among his companions ever thought of calling him a "Miss Nancy," a "muff," or other like names.

No, indeed! and was not Tom Norris the king of Mr. Peters' school, the judge in all disputes, the one to settle all difficulties, to "help a fellow out of a scrape"?

Nora would as soon have thought of questioning her own care and wisdom for Lily as she would that of "Master Tom."

"Miss Lily's all right, ma'am, she's with Master Tom," would be answer enough when there was any inquiry about the little girl; and it was quite satisfactory to mother or nurse to know that she was with her brother. No fear that Lily would come to harm or fall into mischief with Tom to guard and guide her.

So she made no objection when Lily came running to her and begged to be dressed to go out with Tom; and she soon had her ready.

As the little girl went downstairs to join her brother, he stood in the hall below, putting on his overcoat.

"Lily," he said, when he saw her, "did you tell Nora to sew on these two buttons?"

"Oh, Tom!" cried Lily, clasping her hands together, and looking ashamed and troubled, as she well might.

"You told me, Lily," said Tom, "when I wanted to ask mamma to give the order, that you would be sure to attend to it, and that you would go right away and tell Nora. Now you must wait till I go up and have it done. You put it off, I suppose, and so forgot it."

Yes, that was just it; more procrastination, and so forgetfulness.

Tom did not speak angrily, but his voice was grave, and Lily saw that he was vexed.

"I'm so sorry," she said to herself, as she opened the front door, and stood waiting for her brother upon the stoop. "I did mean to remember and tell Nora right away, and I only just stopped to listen to mamma's musical box for a moment, and so I went and forgot. It is too mean I do forget so quick."

What was the reason Lily forgot so quickly and so often?

Because she allowed other things to take her time and her attention from the duty she should first attend to.

"Please, dear little lady, to help a poor woman."

Lily started, and looked around. She had not seen the woman coming, and she now was half way up the steps, almost at her elbow.

"Please, little lady," the woman began again; "I've a little girl at home no bigger nor yourself, and five more of 'em, and not a mouthful to eat have they had these twenty-four hours. A little money to buy bread for 'em, and bless your beautiful face."

"Oh, dear! I'm so sorry," said Lily; not moved by the woman's flattery, but by the vision of the six children no larger than herself, who were starving. "I think mamma would give you lots of things if she were home, but she is not; or papa either. Couldn't you come again?"

"And I might go home to find them dying or dead," whined the old woman, coming nearer, and trying to peer within the half open door. "You couldn't give a poor mother a loaf of bread, or a few pennies, little lady? I'm not a beggar at all; I'd be ashamed to beg, but I thought if I could get a lift this once, I'd work it out some day. I never begged in my life; but there's the children starving, and me with a broken arm."

Lily, who was a charitable and generous child, felt her sympathy strongly roused, and remembering the store in her money-box upstairs, she said,—

"Oh, yes! I have money of my own, and I'll give you some. But it's way upstairs, so you'll have to wait a minute till I bring it. And I'll see if I can have a loaf of bread for you too."

The woman was about to follow her into the house; but Lily, recollecting certain charges she had heard given to the servants, and also a sad and mortifying thing which had once happened to Maggie Bradford, would not suffer her to enter. But, not wishing to hurt the woman's feelings, she said,—

"I think you'd better wait outside. Mamma don't like to have strange people come in when there's no one about; and the servants are all downstairs 'cept Nora, and she's up. I'll be back in a minute;" and, with an encouraging nod to the woman, away she flew on her errand of kindness.

Poor Lily! in the midst of her intended prudence, she had been most imprudent; for she left the door partially open, not wishing to seem too inhospitable, and never dreaming the woman would disregard her order, and take advantage of her absence.

She ran into the nursery and found her money-box, taking from it twenty-five cents. Tom was speaking to Nora, who was still busy with his coat, and Lily did not interrupt him. But presently he turned to her.

"Going to do some shopping too, Lily?" he asked, as he saw what she was doing.

"No," said Lily, "this is for a poor woman downstairs. Don't you want to give her something too, Tom? And do you think mamma would let me give her a loaf of bread? She's not a common beggar: she says she's not; and she has six children, all starving, just about as big as me."

"Miss Lily," said Nora, starting up, "now what have you done with her? Where is she?"

"Oh, you needn't be afraid, Nora," answered Lily. "I was very careful, and told her to stay outside, on the stoop, 'cause I remembered how Maggie let a man come in the house, and how he stole her papa's new overcoat while she went upstairs. I took very good care of her, and told her she couldn't come in, 'cause every one was upstairs or downstairs. Shall you give her some money? and can I have the bread, Tom?"

"Wait till I come down and see the woman," said Tom, who knew that Lily's sympathies were too apt to run away with her judgment.

Lily waited with what patience she might for a moment or two; but it seemed to her that Nora's fingers moved very slowly.

"Tom," she said presently, "couldn't you come and see the woman while Nora finishes the coat? You know those children must be growing starveder and starveder every minute."

Tom laughed, but consented; and, taking her hand, was about to lead her from the room, when Nora stopped her.

"Miss Lily," she said, "you took away my large scissors this morning, and I need them to cut out some work. Will you bring them to me before you go down again?"

"You find them, please, Nora," answered Lily. "They're somewhere in my baby-house."

"Your mamma forbid it," said Nora. "She told me when you took a thing that way and kept it, I was to make you bring it back, and not go and hunt it up for you."

"Just this once," pleaded Lily.

Nora shook her head, though she would herself willingly have humored the child.

"Your mamma was here, you know, when you took the scissors," she said, "and she told me if you did not bring them back as you promised, I was to send you for them. She said you are getting too much in the way of thinking that I am to hunt up all the things you don't put back in their places, and to see to every thing you put off and leave undone. You must bring me the scissors before you go, dear."

"While you find them I'll go down and talk to your woman with the half-dozen children all just of your size," said Tom, who evidently had his doubts on the subject of Lily's protégée; "and if she seems all right you shall give her some food; but we won't give her money till we know more about her. That is mamma's rule, you know. Nora, please bring me the coat when it is done."

And Tom went away, leaving Lily to follow when she had found the scissors.

It took her some three or four minutes to do this; for she had left them among a heap of bits of silk and ribbon with which she had been playing that morning, and neglecting to take the scissors back to Nora when she had finished with them, as she had promised to do, she had forgotten them altogether, and could not find them at once.

The coat was ready when she went back to Nora, and the nurse followed her downstairs with it.

"Your bird had flown when I came down, Lil," said Tom, when he saw her.

"Who, the woman? Had she gone away?" asked Lily.

"Yes, she had gone; no sign of her. But didn't you say you had shut her out?"

"I told her to stay out, 'cause there was no one about in this part of the house to take care of her," answered Lily, with an air of confident wisdom and prudence.

"And did you not shut the door?" asked Tom.

"Not so very tight," said Lily. "I left it a little scrap open, for fear her feelings would be hurt, and maybe she might think I wasn't coming back to her."

"Oh, wise Lily!" said Tom, laughing, as he put on his overcoat; "you left the door standing open, and told her there was no one in this part of the house! Next time, little woman, close the door."

"Did she come in?" asked Lily. "I told her she must not."

"No, I believe not," answered Tom; "and as it is there is no harm done, for I've looked round, and there's nothing touched. The hats and coats are all right, and every thing else seems to be safe. You've had better luck or a better beggar than poor Maggie; but next time, puss, don't you leave any one the chance to walk in when the coast is clear."

"You're sure there's nothing taken, and that she's not in the house, Master Tom?" said prudent Nora.

"Yes, I believe it's all safe," said Tom; "but you'd better call Robert up, and tell him to make a thorough search. Come, Lily, we'll be off now."

III.

THE SILVER INKSTAND.

"LILY," said Tom, as they went down the street together, "don't you see what a lot of trouble your habit of putting off makes for yourself and every one about you?"

"Yes, I should think I did," answered Lily, with energy. "I'm dreadfully sorry about your coat, Tom; I really am, dreadfully."

Apparently her remorse did not affect her spirits much, for, as she spoke, she went skipping along, swinging her brother's hand back and forth, and smiling and nodding with glee.

"I was not speaking for myself so much, or caring about my coat just then," said Tom. "That does not matter now; but this is such a bad habit of yours, Lily, and it is growing worse and worse."

"Oh, but I'm going to begin to cure myself very soon," said Lily. "Maggie and Bessie are going to make me a proverb picture, and Belle is going to help them; and as soon as I have it I will improve myself by it. Tom, why don't the boys in your school make proverb pictures for each other? I should think they would. Proverb pictures are so very interesting, and so improving too, Tom."

"I dare say, when one is willing to be improved," said Tom; "but I do not think our boys would care much about them. They are rather too large for that."

"Dear me! I should think the older people are the better they'd like them," said Lily; "'cause they can make them better when they've learned to draw. I can't make them very fit to be seen yet; but when I'm grown up and can draw nicely, I'll make a whole lot; and when I go to make visits, or my acquaintances come to see me, and I see they have faults or bad habits, I'll just give them a proverb picture to help them to correct themselves."

"If you don't change your mind in the mean time," said Tom, merrily. "I don't think you'll be overrun with visitors if you entertain them in that fashion, Lily. But," becoming grave again, "I want you to listen to me, and seriously, too. You see what trouble this putting off and never being ready in time makes for yourself; and you can't help seeing also how it provokes other people, and good reason, too. For you know, Lily, you have no rightto make such inconvenience for other people."

"Ho!" said Lily. "I see, Tom, you're like Maggie's old Quaker lady, cross old thing! I don't mean you're cross, not one bit; only you think, like her, that somebody has no right to take up other people's time by making them wait."

"What Quaker lady?" asked Tom.

Lily repeated Maggie's story, almost word for word, as she had told it. Tom was very much amused, but he did not let Lily see that; for it was hard to make her talk seriously on any subject, and he did not wish to have her see him laugh just now.

"Yes," he said, with all the gravity he could muster, "I am much of the opinion of that old lady. I do not think that any one has the right to waste the time of other people, by keeping them waiting, when it can be avoided; or by failing to do that which they are expected, or perhaps have promised, to do. I know a lady—"

"What's her name?" questioned Lily.

"Never mind her name. I know a lady who is never ready at the time for which she makes an engagement, and who in this way makes herself a nuisance to all who are obliged to have any business with her; who always comes into church when the service is half over; who is late at every meal, either in her own house, or other people's—"

"Yes," said Lily; "and don't you remember, Tom, how mad papa was that time she came to dinner at our house when Mr. Francis was there; and he and papa had a very important engagement, and she kept the dinner waiting so long that they could not get to their engagement in time; and wasn't papa mad?"

"Not mad exactly," said Tom, "but he was very much vexed, and with reason; but I see you know whom I mean, Lily."

"Oh, yes, very well indeed; you mean Miss Lee. She's just too provoking for any thing; but then I never mean to be like her. Pretty soon I'm going to begin to correct myself of putting off, and not being ready in time."

"But why don't you begin now, right off?" said Tom.

"Would you?" asked Lily, doubtfully. "I thought I'd wait till I had the proverb picture."

"Yes, begin to-day, this very minute," said Tom.

"There's nothing for me to put off just now," said Lily.

"I mean make up your mind; take a resolution you will begin at once," said Tom. "You see, Lily, it is the same in every thing. You always think, 'it is time enough,' or 'another time will do;' and so the thing is left undone, or you make some trouble. You are a real generous, obliging little girl, but you could be far more helpful if you had not this bad habit. Mamma often asks you to do some little thing for her; but if she trusts to you, ten to one—"

Lily stopped short where she stood, with a face of the blankest dismay, and interrupted her brother in a distressed voice.

"Oh, Tom!" she said. "I did do such a thing! Mamma did trust me, and I've done such a thing, and never did it."

"What is it? What have you done, and what haven't you done?" asked Tom, rather at a loss to understand her, as you may imagine he would be.

"Mamma was just going out with Mrs. Bradford, when a note came she had to answer before she went," said Lily; "and she was in a great hurry, and so she told me to be a help to her, and put away all her writing things very carefully. And I said I would, and she trusted me, and told me to do it right away, and — and — oh, Tom!"

"And you did not do it," said Tom, gravely. "You did not do it at once, but put it off, and so left it undone."

"Yes," answered Lily, her eyes filling, and her voice shaking. "I never did it, and I should think I was provoking. I should think the whole world might be provoked with me. Tom, I ought to go back; but you oughtn't to be kept for me any longer. You can take me to our house, and just leave me; and I'll go right in, and put away mamma's things, and stay at home for a punishment to myself, and to make me see how troublesome putting off is."

"Mamma's things are all put away, Lily," said Tom.

"Who did it? You?" asked Lily, recovering her spirits a little.

"Yes. I did not know you had promised to do it, or I should have spoken to you about it; but when I was looking round to see if that beggar woman had been at any mischief, I saw mamma's writing things lying about over the table, and her desk open; so I just put every thing away, and locked the desk. It is all right now," added Tom, believing it was as he said. "But how came you to forget mamma's orders, Lily?"

"It was all the fault of that old monkey," said Lily, as her brother led her on. "Horrid thing! I wish he'd stayed away, and that I hadn't looked at him, or given him cakes or pennies or any thing. His frock was awfully dirty too," she added, forgetting all the amusement the monkey had afforded her, and now only disposed to regard him as the cause of her neglect of her mother's wishes.

"I should not blame the poor monkey if I were you," said Tom. "How was it? You went to look at the monkey in place of attending to mamma's orders, and so forgot all about them?"

"Yes," said Lily. "I meant to look at him for only one minute, and then to put away the things just as mamma told me, but he was so funny I forgot; and then the puppies came; and that's the way I never remembered them at all."

"Well, you see," said Tom, "you should have put away mamma's things at once, and then gone to look at the monkey. And it was your own fault, not the monkey's, Lily. He did not ask you to come and look at him; it was your own choice."

"Yes," answered Lily, rather meekly for her.

"Now can't you see it is better for you to begin at once?" said Tom. "Don't let Procrastination hinder you here, Lil. The old fellow don't want himself put down, and will trump up all manner of excuses to keep his hold on you. But you root him up just as quick as you can. Begin this very day; and the next time you have any thing to do, don't listen to one of his fine speeches."

"Yes, so I will, I b'lieve," said Lily. "I won't wait for the proverb picture, but just begin to-day. I wish there would come something I want to put off, and I wouldn't put it off, but just do it very quick indeed."

Poor Lily! She was to learn more that day of the evils of procrastination in her own case.

Tom thought he had said enough to her now; and they went on together to the store where he wished to buy his dog-house. Here they chose one, and here also they purchased a collar for the puppy, Tom allowing Lily to pick out a red one, although he would himself have preferred blue. Was he not a kind brother?

As they were on their way home, they met Maggie and Bessie Bradford, with their Aunt Annie.

Lily rushed forward, letting go her hold on her brother's hand; and Maggie ran to meet her, almost as eager as she was.

"Is my proverb picture nearly ready?" asked Lily.

"Yes, quite," answered Maggie; "and we want you to come to our house, so we can explain it to you. We've just been to your house to ask you, but you were out, or else you could have come to take tea with us, if your mamma had said so. I wonder if she wouldn't just as lief you should come now. Can't Lily come with us, Tom?"

Tom had now come up to the little girls, and so had Miss Annie Stanton and Bessie; and, after taking off his hat to the young lady, he answered, —

"I think not to-night, Maggie. At least I do not like to take it upon myself to give her leave; for she had a bad sore throat yesterday, and I do not think mamma would like to have her out in the evening air."

Lily looked as if she were about to cry, and Maggie and Bessie also looked disappointed.

"Never mind," said Bessie, cheering up in one moment; "it will be just as good if you come to-morrow and spend the day. Mamma said we could ask you to do that if you could not come this afternoon; and we will have you a longer time, Lily."

"That's putting off, though," said Lily, with a pout, "and I've just made up my mind not to do it."

Tom laughed, and so did Miss Annie, both somewhat amused at Lily's haste to practise the new virtue as soon as it fell in with her own wishes; but Maggie and Bessie thought this a very sensible view of the matter.

"But one may put off a thing when it comes in the way of a duty, or of another thing which should be attended to first," said Annie Stanton. "When mamma's wishes and your pleasure come in the way of one another, which should you put first?"

"Why, what mamma wishes, Miss Annie. I should think I would do what mamma wants first. Anyway I ought to would" added Lily, thinking of her shortcomings of that very day.

"Then you see you may put off coming to Maggie and Bessie till to-morrow, since your mamma does not wish you to be out at night," said Miss Stanton; and with this agreement, the little friends parted.

"I see," said Lily, demurely, but with a gleam of mischief in her eye, — "I see people don't think it is as much harm to put off things you want to do as it is to put off what you don't want to do."

"Well," said Tom, smiling, "you see that is where it is, Lil. We are so apt to think it will do to put off what we do not care to do very much, — any little duty or task; but if it is some pleasure, we are generally ready enough to do it at once."

"Maggie thinks I put off pleasures too," said Lily. "She was real provoked with me 'cause I kept them waiting to go to the party the other day."

"Do you like other people to keep you waiting, Lily?"

"No, indeed, I don't," said Lily.

"Then ought you not to be careful how you do it to others?"

"Yes, I know, Tom, and I don't mean to do it; but somehow I do. But now you see if I do not improve myself a good deal of this habit," said Lily, confidently, yet carelessly; for it was plainly to be seen that she thought this vexatious fault of but little consequence.

Lily had meant to confess to her mother how neglectful she had been of her wishes; but when she and Tom reached home, they found with Mrs. Norris a lady who had been invited to dinner. So Lily thought she would postpone her confession until by and by, and not draw upon herself her mother's grave and reproachful look in the presence of company.

I do not know that she was to blame for this. Few little girls but would have done the same, I think; and Lily had no idea that any mischief or loss had come from her procrastination.

Dinner was over, Tom gone upstairs to prepare his lessons for to-morrow, and Lily, in her favorite evening seat,—that is, perched upon the arm of her father's chair while he read his paper,—was happily playing with some paper dolls, while mamma and her friend sat opposite, talking, when a person came with a message requiring an immediate answer.

Mrs. Norris went to her secretary and wrote the note, using for the purpose an ordinary inkstand which belonged there; and then said approvingly to Lily,—

"My pet, how nicely you put away mamma's writing things; all the papers in their proper places and order. Pretty well done for such a little girl."

"Mamma," said Lily, wishing that she need not speak before Miss Hamilton, but too honest to take credit which was not her just due,—"Mamma, I did not put them away; it was Tom. I—I—forgot, mamma. I waited to look at a monkey before I put them away, and then the puppy came, and Tom took me out; and I forgot all about your things, and how I had promised, and never remembered till we were out in the street; and then Tom told me he had put them away, but he didn't know you had told me to do it."

It was all out now; and Lily, as she glanced at Miss Hamilton, felt as if she could not be thankful enough to that lady for seeming so absorbed in the photograph album she was turning over.

Mrs. Norris uttered no word of reproach; but, as she looked within the well-ordered secretary, she said,—

"Where did Tom put the silver inkstand? I do not see it."

"I don't know, mamma," answered Lily. "Is it not there? Tom said he came in here and saw your things lying on the table, and he thought you must have forgotten them, so he put them all away. Shall I go and ask him what he did with the inkstand?"

"No," said her mother, "I do not wish to disturb him at his lessons. I will look further."

But further search proved vain, though Mrs. Norris looked, not only through each nook and partition of the secretary, but also all over the room. Still she was not at all disturbed at the non-appearance of the inkstand.

"Send up and ask Tom, my dear," said Mr. Norris.

"Oh, it is not necessary," said his wife. "He may have put it in some unusual place. If he took care of it, it is quite safe. He will be down presently, and I do not care to interrupt him."

"See what it is to have a good character, Lily," said her father, passing his arm about the little figure on the arm of his chair, and smiling into the rosy mischievous face before him. "How long before mamma will be able to put such trust in you, do you think?"

"Oh, very soon, papa; you'll see," said Lily, confident in the strength of her newly formed resolution.

It was not long before Tom made good his mother's words by appearing, his lessons all ready for the next day, for it happened that he had not had much to do that evening; and Mrs. Norris immediately asked him, —

"What did you do with my silver inkstand, my boy?"

"I did not have it, mamma," was the answer.

"But you put it away this afternoon, did you not?"

"No," answered Tom, wonderingly, but positively.

"Why, yes, Tom," said Lily, "you told me you had put away all mamma's things that she left on the table."

"But there was no inkstand there," said Tom. "I remember noticing that, because I said to myself, 'Mamma has taken time to put by her ink;' and I supposed you had feared it would be spilled, mamma. There was no inkstand upon the table, I am sure."

"Did you move the inkstand at all, Lily?" asked Mrs. Norris.

"No, mamma, I never touched it. I did not put away one single thing."

Tom helped his mother in a fresh search for the missing inkstand; but all in vain.

Then the servant man was called, and questioned.

"I saw Miss Lily with her hand on the inkstand when I called her to see the little dogs this afternoon, ma'am," he said, in reply to Mrs. Norris's inquiries. "Do you remember, if you please, Miss Lily?"

"Oh, yes," said Lily. "I remember now, mamma. I did take it up to put it away, but I set it down again when I ran after Robert to see the puppies. I meant to come right back, but I never thought of it again."

"Master Tom," said Robert, "you were asking me had I seen a beggar-woman about the door this afternoon. Could she have been in here, and caught up the inkstand? If she'd just opened the library door, and peeped in, it would have been the first thing she'd see, for it stood right here, where Miss Lily left it."

Tom looked dismayed, and Lily still more so; for, if the inkstand were indeed stolen, was it not all her fault? Owing to her procrastination, to the putting off of the small service her mother had asked of her? And so it proved; for nothing could be found of the inkstand, and it was never heard of again. Its loss could be accounted for in no other way than by supposing that the woman, finding the door left open, and learning from Lily's imprudent words that there was no one about to interfere with her, had walked in, opened the library door, and seeing the inkstand, had snatched it up, and made off with it.

Lily's shame and grief were very great, all the more so because she knew that this inkstand was dearly loved and valued by her mamma, because it had been the gift of a dead sister. And seeing this, her mother could not bear to reproach her, for it was very unusual for Lily to take her own wrong-doing much to heart. But this was, as she said herself, "the worst consequence I ever did in all my long life;" and she probably felt it all the more deeply for her kind mother's forbearance.

That she was sufficiently punished by her own remorse was plainly to be seen; and long after she was in bed and fast asleep, her mother heard long sobs heaving her little breast, and found her pillow all wet with tears.

"My poor little one! I hope it may be a lasting lesson to her," said the mother, as she pushed back the hair from the flushed and tear-stained face. "If it should be, I shall think it cheaply purchased even by the loss of my much valued inkstand."

IV

LILY'S PROVERB PICTURE.

LILY was still in a very subdued and melancholy frame of mind when she reached the Bradfords' house on the following day; and when her little playmates inquired the cause, she made answer, —

"If mamma had given me my deservings, she would have shut me up in a room by myself, and never let me come out in all my life, nor come to spend the day with you any more. It's a great deal too good for such a sinner as me, and something ought to be done to me. I don't mean to have a nice time to-day."

This virtuous resolution was forgotten, however, before the day was over; but at the time it much astonished her young friends, as did also the low state of Lily's spirits.

Fresh questions followed; and Lily told her story, mingling her own bitter self-accusations with reproaches against the supposed thief.

"For I told her she was not to come in, 'cause there was no one about to 'tend to her," she said, as if this were an added aggravation of her sorrows; "and I only left the door open for fear her feelings would be hurt; but now I don't b'lieve she had any to hurt. I don't s'pose thieves have many feelings, do you, Maggie?"

"No, I don't believe they have," answered Maggie. "I just expect their feelings are 'lost to sight, and not to memory dear.'"

This fine sentiment, having been properly appreciated, called up the recollection of the promised proverb picture.

"Did you find a proverb that would be a lesson for me, or did you have to make one?" asked mournful Lily.

"Mamma told us one," said Maggie. "It is 'Procrastination is the thief of Time.'"

"You'd better say the thief of inkstands," said Lily, ruefully. "Maggie and Bessie and Belle, I feel 'most as if it was me who had stolen mamma's inkstand."

The other little girls all set about consoling her; and Bessie took an opportunity to whisper to Maggie that she thought they had better not give Lily the proverb picture that day because it might make her feel worse.

But this was not by any means Lily's view of the matter; and she presently asked to be shown this joint production of her three little friends, Maggie and Bessie and Belle.

Accordingly, the picture, or rather pictures, were brought forth, and with them the poem which Maggie had composed to accompany them.

When the red ribbon which tied the first was taken off, and the pictures unrolled, they proved quite a panorama; and Lily's mournful face lighted up at the sight.

"How good of you!" she said. "It must have taken you ever so long to draw all those pictures."

"There are four of them," said Bessie. "Belle made two, 'cause she can draw the best, and Maggie made one, and I one; but Maggie made 'most all the ideas. I think they're so very plain you can make them out for yourself, Lily, but we'll 'splain them to you if you like."

"I'll see how much I can find out, and you can tell me the rest," said Lily, setting herself at once to the study of the drawings.

"What's the reading on this one?" she asked. "P-r-o-pro-c-r-a-s-cras—Oh! I s'pose this is 'Procrastination is the thief of Time.'"

"Yes," said Maggie.

"And this is a skeleton," said Lily, "a skeleton with a goblet in one hand, and a—and a"—Lily hesitated, wishing to be sure to hit the right nail on the head—"and a—I'm not quite sure if it's a feather dust-brush, or a coachman's whip."

"Oh!" exclaimed Belle, indignant.

"Why, Lily!" said Bessie, "that's Time with his hour-glass and scythe, and Belle drew that picture, and we think it's the very best one of all."

"I'm sorry," said Lily, rather ashamed of not having at once recognized the articles in question.

"You know in the pictures Time is always a very thin old man," said Bessie, "so we had to make him so to have it real; and Maggie told Belle she'd better make him as thin as she could, 'cause that horrid thief Procrastination bothers him so he hardly has any flesh on his bones. This is a kind of allegory picture, you see, Lily."

"Yes, I understand. And this rather beggar-looking child—" Lily hesitated again, unwilling to run the risk of making any more such uncomplimentary mistakes. "I think you'd better tell me about it. I'm 'fraid I'm rather stupid this morning. I think I went crazy last night about that inkstand, and I'm hardly recovered yet. I b'lieve that's the reason I didn't know Time's hour-glass and scythe at first."

Never before had her little friends known Lily to speak and look with such solemnity, and they all felt very much for her.

Maggie, however, thought it well to improve the occasion.

"I did not want to seem severe with her," she said afterward to Bessie and Belle, "but I thought the picture might make a deeper impression if I let her see to what a dreadful condition procrastinating people might come."

"Yes," she said to Lily, "yes, that is Procrastination, all ragged and dirty and starved. He never has a nice time, and he hardly ever has any thing to eat, 'cause when people say to him, 'Procrastination, dinner is ready,' he says, 'I think I'll eat by and by;' and then when he comes, the dinner is all gone, and he has to go hungry: and when they say, 'Go and get washed, and have on clean clothes,' he says, 'Another day I will;' so he becomes all ragged, and his friends are so ashamed of him that they just let him take care of himself. That's the way he looks so horridly. And poor old Time hardly knows what to do with himself for the way that troublesome fellow worries him. He doesn't leave Time alone to do his duty one minute. Do you see these things in Procrastination's hand?"

"Yes; what are they?" asked Lily, deeply interested.

"They are Time's purse and pocket handkerchief that Procrastination—I think we'd better call him Pro, because it takes so long to say Procrastination—that Pro has stolen out of his pocket; and here at his feet are some broken hour-glasses; and now he is running after Time, and trying to steal his last hour-glass, so that the poor old fellow will have none left. That means, when you're not talking allegory, that Pro steals the hours and makes you lose all your time; but he can not catch him up, which means that when you have lost your time, you never can catch up with it."

"Yes," said Lily, dolefully; "but I think it would be better if you made Pro stealing inkstands. It's just what I deserve. Is that all about that picture?"

"Yes," answered Maggie; "now we come to real life. Bessie, this is your picture; tell Lily about it."

It is to be observed that the ragged figure which represented Procrastination, or "Pro," was to be seen in each successive picture. This was considered a judicious mingling of the allegorical with reality.

"This," said Bessie, "is a little girl whose mamma said to her, 'My dear, there is a match upon the carpet; pick it up right away.' But Procrastination"—Bessie would not on any account have shortened her words, especially on such a grave occasion—"came and whispered to her, 'By and by will do; it's time enough;' and presently her little sister came in and picked up the match, and set herself on fire, and she was quite burnt up before she could be put out, and she was the only sister the put-offing child had, and she stayed unhappy all the rest of the days of her life."

"Like me," said Lily.

"Oh, no," said Maggie, cheerfully, "you'll get over that inkstand. I find people generally do get over things; at least, I do. Take courage by me, Lily. I thought I never should recover having papa's coat stolen, but you see I have; and I think I'm about as happy as any child could be."

"Ah! but you wasn't disobedient, and didn't put off," said Lily. "Tell me some more."

"Perhaps we'd better not, 'cause you feel so badly," said Bessie.

"They do me good," answered Lily. "I don't think I can care for any thing else to-day. Who made this picture?"

"I did," said Maggie, "and this is the story of it. This is fable or allegory too;" and, unrolling another sheet of paper, Maggie read aloud her famous poem, which had been pronounced a great success by both Bessie and Belle. Her picture consisted of a series of small drawings, which explained themselves as she read the verses.

"There's a bad little fellow,

His name it is Pro-

Cras-tin-a-ti-on;

And to you I will show

How he robs and he steals

And he plagues Father Time.

I'll tell you all this,

And I'll tell you in rhyme.

When to school he is sent,

He most slowly doth go,

For he stops first to play,

Then to look at some show;

By the hour he is there,

Why! the school is 'most out.

That's one way he robs Time,

This sad putting-off lout.

When his mother doth say,

'Go this errand for me,'

He will say, 'By and by;'

'Pretty soon;' 'I will see;'

29

Till at last 'tis too late,
Or his mother must go.
'Tis a base, heartless crime,
For a child to do so.
But there's worse yet to tell,
For to church he goes late;
And he reaches God's house
In a sad, dirty state;
For he never is dressed,
And he never is clean.
That 'tis all putting off,
Is quite plain to be seen.
He ne'er has a book,
Or a toy, or a pet,
For to put them away
He doth always forget;
So they're broken or lost,
Or most shamefully torn;
And he's nothing to do,
Which is very forlorn.
Take heed now, ye children,
And list to my tale;
What e'er you've to do,
Do at once, without fail;
For if you'd be happy,
And useful, and gay,
Don't put off till to-morrow
The work of to-day.
Remember, 'tis minutes
That make up the hours;

As the small, tiny seeds

Bring the beautiful flowers.

Don't procrastinate then,

O ye daughters of earth!

For woman's but grass

From the day of her birth."

In the ears of the little listeners this was a perfect gem of poetry, far beyond any thing Maggie had ever written before, whether it were "divine song," or "moral poem." The concluding lines were considered particularly fine, and, indeed, had been added on account of their striking effect.

Bessie and Belle had heard it before, but they listened with rapt attention, and Lily was very much impressed. The third verse she felt particularly adapted to her case, though Maggie had intended no home thrust when she wrote it. But, to Lily's mind, it just suited the affair of the inkstand; and when Maggie finished reading, she exclaimed, —

"I should think I was a base, heartless crime!"

The children all hastened to console her, and to assure her that they thought she would not fail to improve, now that she saw her fault so plainly.

"I didn't mean that the child in the poem was really you," said Maggie. "That's the reason I made Pro a boy instead of a girl. I only wanted to show you what people might come to who procrastinated all the time, and never were punctual."

Maggie's drawing, as you have heard, was divided up into a number of smaller pictures, each one suited to a particular verse of the poem; and they explained themselves to one who had read or heard the latter.

The fourth and last picture had been drawn by Belle, the chief artist among the little party.

This also represented Father Time, who had now grown fat and flourishing, which was somewhat singular under the circumstances. He was accompanied by another burly figure, and both were armed with many lashes and whips with which they chased "Pro," now himself reduced to a skeleton state, and vainly endeavoring to escape from his tormentors.

"This," said Belle, "is my drawing, but it is Maggie's idea, and Bessie and I think it is pretty grand. Here is that naughty Pro, and he has lost every thing and every one he had in the world, all through his own putting off; and here," pointing to little dots and round o's with which the page was covered, "here are the hours and minutes flying away from him too. The largest ones are the hours; the little ones, the minutes. And here are Father Time and Remorse coming after him with their — their — What kind of whips do they have, Maggie?"

"Scorpion whips," answered Maggie. "It was a very convenient thing that I happened to read the other day about the 'scorpion whip of Remorse,' and it just gave me the idea for this picture. It means that when we feel very badly about something we know we deserve, it is just as bad as the stings of scorpions and bugs and other horrid things. And I thought we'd make believe Remorse had two scorpion whips, and lent one to Time to chase Procrastination with."

"Here's the ocean," said Belle, directing Lily's attention to where high, curling waves were supposed to be leaping and dashing upward, "and Pro was running away so fast from those dreadful scorpion whips that he never saw it, but ran right into the water, and was drowned; and that was the end ofhim."

Belle's tone was very triumphant when she uttered the last word, as though she were glad to have thus disposed of a troublesome customer.

"I'm sure," said Lily, with an air of melancholy satisfaction, "I'm sure I'm very much obliged to you all for taking so much trouble to improve me; and I don't see how I can help being better now."

"Then that's all we ask," said Maggie, "and we shan't regret any trouble we took. Now let's go and play."

If the other children had had any fears that Lily's remorse and the "lesson" they had given her would interfere with her enjoyment of the day, such fears were soon put to flight; for in ten minutes she was as merry and roguish as ever, and quite disposed to join in all the entertainment provided for her.

V.

PROMISING.

"HOW many of my little girls would like to help in a good work?" asked Miss Ashton, some two or three days after this.

Ten little hands went up. Ten? Nay, I think there were thirteen or fourteen; for some of the children were not content with holding up one, but raised both in their zeal to show Miss Ashton they were ready to do what she asked.

Miss Ashton went on to explain.

"I think you will all remember," she said, "the lame soldier who was run over and killed on the corner of this street?"

There was a murmur of assenting voices, and little Belle added,—

"Papa said it was a very generous thing for you and Mrs. Ashton to take care of his three children, Miss Ashton; and I think so too."

Miss Ashton smiled at her, and continued,—

"But we could not take care of them always, dear Belle, and through the kindness of some friends we have found a pleasant home in the country for them. It is necessary that they should be comfortably fitted out before we send them there, however, and my uncle says that he will provide all the materials that the school will make up. The young ladies in my mother's room say they will make all the dresses and more difficult garments, and leave the simple and easier ones for you, if you choose to help. But before you make any promises, I wish you to ask your parents' permission, and also to make up your minds to have the garment you take finished by the end of two weeks, when the children are to leave for their new home. You nearly all sew well enough to do the easy work upon these little skirts and aprons, and I think your friends at home will give you what help you may need."

"But, Miss Ashton," said little Belle, with woe-begone voice and look, "I can hardly sew at all. Aunt Margaret has just begun to teach me, and she says I do take pains, but I b'lieve I do it pretty badly yet."

"And I don't know how to sew," said her cousin, Mabel Walton, who now was sorry that she had always obstinately refused to learn how to use a needle.

"I think we can find some easy thing for you both to do," said Miss Ashton, kindly. "But remember, dear children, what you promise, you must perform. If you undertake this work, you must have it finished at the end of the time I have named,—two weeks. I do not ask you to do it, for the older girls are willing to do all the work; but I thought it might be a pleasure to you to help."

"Oh, yes! indeed it will, Miss Ashton," said Lily, "and I'd like to have two clothes to make. Mamma says I can sew pretty well fur such a little girl, and Nora will show me how."

"One garment will be enough for you, Lily," said Miss Ashton; "if you finish that in time, it is all we shall need."

"You need not be afraid I won't have it done in time, Miss Ashton," said Lily. "I don't put off any more, nor be unpunctual either. I've been early at school every morning this week,"—this was Tuesday,—"and mamma said I was beginning to improve. I couldn't help it very well, I had such a horrid lesson about an old beggar-woman who was nothing but a thief; and then Maggie and Bessie and Belle made me lovely proverb pictures about the consequences of procrastination, and Maggie wrote a splendid poem, so I ought to learn better with all that."

"I think so," said Miss Ashton; "but, by the way, I wonder if Maggie and Bessie would not like to join us in this work. They always take such an interest in all that goes on among us here that perhaps they would be pleased if we offered to let them help."

"Yes, I know they would," cried Belle, always ready to speak in praise of her beloved little playmates. "I know they would. Maggie and Bessie are very full of good works; and they always like to do what we do, if they can, too."

"Very well," said Miss Ashton. "You can ask them when you see them, Belle; and if they would like to help us, tell them to come in to-morrow, at the close of school. You can all bring me word then if your parents are willing for you to undertake this work, and I will give each one a piece to take home."

The next morning each little girl brought word that she had received permission to take home and make such a garment as Miss Ashton should see fit to give her; and they had all been promised help and teaching by their mammas or other friends.

The curiosity and interest of the class having been much excited by Lily's glowing account of the "proverb picture" and poem furnished her by Maggie, Bessie, and Belle, she had been persuaded to bring them with her; and being punctual for the third morning, she exhibited them before school was opened, to the great satisfaction and delight of the other children. They were also displayed to Miss Ashton.

"Maggie is quite a Murphy, isn't she, Miss Ashton?" said Lily.

"A what, dear?" asked the young lady, much puzzled.

"A Murphy—a M-m-ur-phy," said Lily, putting severe and long emphasis on the word, as she saw that her teacher did not yet understand. "Don't you know what a Murphy is, Miss Ashton? It means some one very wise and good, who teaches right things."

"Oh!" said Miss Ashton, smiling, as light broke in upon her; "you mean a Mentor, do you not, Lily?"

"Oh, yes, that's it," said Lily; "but I thought it was Murphy. But I think Murphy is just as pretty a name as Mentor."

"But people would understand your meaning better if you put the right name, Lily," said Miss Ashton, as she rang the bell for silence.

Maggie and Bessie had told Belle that they would be very glad to join in the work of making clothes for the poor little orphans; and accordingly, when school was over and word was brought that they were below, she was sent to bring them up to the school-room. Places were soon found for them among their former school-mates, who were all delighted to see them; and, as Bessie said, "it seemed quite as if they were all young again."

Then Miss Ashton had a large basket of work brought in, and took from it a number of little garments cut out, but not made, which she laid upon the table before her.

"I have six skirts and six aprons here," she said, "and three calico bags, which our little orphans must have to hold their lesson-books. I think we had better give the bags to those who are the youngest, or the least accustomed to sewing, — Bessie, Belle, and Mabel. Then the rest may choose, so far as you can, whether you will take a petticoat or an apron; but as there is more work upon the petticoats than upon the aprons, I shall think it wiser for those who are not very industrious and persevering to take the latter, so that they may be sure to finish their work. Or perhaps the older ones, Nellie, Maggie, Grace, and Dora, might take the skirts, and let the other five take aprons. As I said yesterday, the young ladies in the other room will finish whatever you leave."

All were satisfied with this arrangement but two.

"Miss Ashton," said Nellie Ransom, in rather a hesitating voice, as though she thought she might be drawing upon herself the disapproval of her classmates, — "Miss Ashton, I think perhaps I had better only take an apron. I do not sew very fast, and I might not have a skirt done in time; and I would rather take the apron, so that I may be sure to finish it."

"Pooh!" said Lily, "I should think any one might have a petticoat done in two weeks! No, not pooh, either, Nellie, I forgot that was not courteous; but then I should think you'd have plenty of time to make the skirt, and I'm going to take one 'stead of the apron, if Miss Ashton will let me."

"I will let you," said her teacher. "I told you you should take what you pleased; but, Lily, I think Nellie is a wise little girl not to undertake more than she feels sure she can do, and you would do well to follow her example. You do not like steady work, you know, Lily, and I should not wish the petticoat to be brought back to me half finished."

"Oh, I'd never do that!" exclaimed Lily. "I see, Miss Ashton, you think it probalal that Nellie and I will be the hare and the tortoise,—Nellie the tortoise and I the hare; but we'll be two tortoises, won't we, Nellie? And please let me have the petticoat, Miss Ashton. I'll be sure, oh, sure to have it finished!"

Miss Ashton did as she was asked, and handed Lily the skirt; but she looked as if she were not quite so sure that Lily would perform all she promised; and though she smiled as she gave the parcel to the little girl, she shook her head doubtfully, and said,—

"Be careful, Lily, and do not put off till to morrow the task you should do to-day."

"No, ma'am," answered Lily, confidently, "I am quite cured of that. I wish you'd let me have two just to see how soon I will have them finished."

"If you finish the petticoat at the end of ten days, you shall have some other thing to make," said Miss Ashton, rather gravely. "Nellie, my dear, here is your apron."

The work was very neatly cut out and basted; prepared so that the little girls might not find it difficult to do, or give more trouble than was actually necessary to their friends at home; and each one opened her parcel and examined it with great satisfaction after they were dismissed.

"I expect Nellie's will be sewed the best, 'cause she takes so much pains with every thing she does," said Bessie. "Hers and Dora's will be, for Dora is industrious too, and has a great deal of perseverance."

"I think mine will be the best," said Gracie, "for I sew very nicely. Mrs. Bradish told mamma she never saw a child of my age sew so neatly."

"Proudy!" said Lily, "you always think you do every thing better than anybody else; and you always go and tell when any one makes you a compliment. Gracie, you do grow conceiteder and conceiteder every day. Pretty soon, we won't be able to stand you at all."

"Why, Lily!" said Belle, "you're a dreadful anti-politer this morning."

"I don't care," said Lily; "Gracie does make me so mad. Yes, I do care about being called an anti-politer too," she added on second thoughts; "but, Gracie, I don't believe your work will be the best. I think like Bessie, that Nellie's will be, 'cause she sews so nicely; and so does Maggie."

"Anyhow mine will be done, and yours won't, I know," retorted Gracie, who always resented very strongly the idea that any other child could do as well or better than herself. "You always put off and procrastinate, so that you never have any thing ready at the right time."

"Well, I'm not going to do so any more," said Lily; "and, anyhow, I'd rather be Pro than Proudy. It's very, very naughty to be proud, and it's only a—a—well, an inconvenient habit to procrastinate. And I'm pretty well cured of it now. Don't you be afraid my petticoat won't be done; and don't let's be cross about it any more, Gracie."

Peace was restored by her last words; but here were Lily's snares and stumbling-blocks. Firstly, that she had too much confidence in her own strength, and was too sure that she could cure herself of this troublesome habit if she only chose to do so; secondly, that she hardly looked upon it as a fault at all, and did not think it of much consequence, except just at the moment when it had brought some great annoyance upon herself or others.

Lily was gay, light-hearted, and sweet-tempered, and trouble or disappointment seldom oppressed her spirits long,—all good things and great blessings in their proper times and places; but she sometimes let this run into carelessness, and was often disposed to make too light of her faults and their consequences. She certainly had warning and help enough in this case, if that were all she needed.

She, Maggie and Bessie, Belle and Mabel all took the same way homeward; and just before they parted, Maggie said,—

"I have an idea! Would it not be a good plan for us five to have a little sewing meeting at our house for these clothes, if mamma has no objections? And it will seem to help us along, and not let it be so stupid; for I do hate to sew."

The other children agreed that it would be a capital arrangement; and Maggie, turning to Bessie, asked if she thought mamma would be willing.

"For we better not make too many plans about it till we know what mamma would say," said Maggie, "or we might 'live in hope only to die in despair.'"

Bessie thought mamma would be quite willing, but agreed with Maggie that it would be better not to build up too many arrangements on this till they knew what she had to say.

"I would like to have asked all the class," said Maggie, "but I do not think mamma wants a great many children about now; because grandmamma's house is being painted, and she and Aunt Annie and Uncle Ruthven and Aunt Bessie are all staying with us, and it makes a pretty large family,—a lovely large one," she added, with a nod of satisfaction in the present size of the household.

"We'll ask mamma if we can have a meeting once a week till our things are all finished," said Bessie; "and we can sew on them between times, and show each other how much we have done. And it may be a little help to you in not putting off, Lily," she said, rather anxiously. "I would be so sorry if your petticoat was not finished."

"Oh, never fear," said Lily; "you are all so afraid about me; and I tell you, I'm not going to put off any more."

"I am sorry, my daughter, that you took the petticoat instead of the apron," said Mrs. Norris, when Lily reached home and told her story of the morning's business. "There would have been more hope of your finishing the apron, with your unsteady ways about work and duties."

"It is not a duty for me to make this, is it, mamma?" asked Lily, unrolling the parcel and holding up the skirt.

"Yes, it is a duty for you to do that which you have promised to do, is it not?"

"Yes, mamma; but I need not have promised if I did not choose."

"No, you need not; but now that you have undertaken it of your own free will, that makes it all the more a duty for you to finish it in time. Will you sew on it a little while this afternoon, after you have had your lunch?"

"No, mamma, I think not," said Lily. "Maggie and Bessie are going to ask their mamma if they can have us for a sewing meeting at their house, and I'll wait and see what they say. It will be fun."

Mrs. Norris sighed as Lily gleefully rolled up her work and tossed it upon the table. This was not a very good beginning.

"Put it away in the large work-box, dear," she said.

"Presently, mamma; I'm just going to tell Nora about it."

"No, Lily, put it away at once. And remember, my darling, that I shall not allow Nora to finish it for you if you fall behindhand through your own fault."

"Oh, no, mamma," said Lily, as she obeyed her mother's order; "but I would have put it away in a minute or two."

VI

BUT NOT PERFORMING.

YOU will readily believe that Lily's "by and by" was long in coming, as it had often been before; and this although her mamma and nurse both invited her more than once to come and begin her petticoat.

The evening brought a note from Maggie Bradford, which was as follows: —

"DEAR LILY,—Mamma says we may have the sewing meeting, and Aunt Annie says she will take care of it up in her room, which is very kind of her; do you not think so? When Baby Annie heard us talking about it, she said, "Me too;" and we told her she should come if she would be good. Mamma says she is afraid she will be a disturbance, but she is so cunning that Bessie and I could not bear to tell her no; and we will be very industrious, even if baby is funny. We make you a life-member of our society for two weeks, till we have the clothes all finished; and we will have a meeting every Thursday afternoon. Come at three o'clock; and Aunt Annie will tell us stories or read to us till four, while we sew, and then we will put away our work and play.

"Yours respectfully and affectionately,

"MAGGIE STANTON BRADFORD.

"P. S. Bessie says of course you'd never think of such a thing as bringing 'Pro' to the meeting. We wouldn't believe it of you; but if you did, we should 'speed the parting guest,' which means to turn him out as quick as you can."

"Maggie knows so many proverbs and wise speeches, and always knows how to make a good use of them," said Lily, when Tom finished reading this epistle to her, she having been in too much haste to try to spell it out for herself. "Now, Tom, what are you laughing at?"

"Why, I'm sure that is a good joke of Maggie's, and well worth being amused at," said Tom.

"Oh, yes," said Lily, "she is very smart, and very funny too. I'm so glad we are going to have the sewing meeting; and, indeed, I don't take 'Pro' with me."

"I am afraid he has paid us a visit this afternoon, Lily," said Mrs. Norris.

"Why, no, dear mamma; at least, I only thought I would wait till I heard what we were going to do at the meeting, and not begin before them. It is nicer to begin all together."

"And I think you will find that all the other children have commenced their work to-day," said Mrs. Norris. "But we shall see."

Lily's mamma was nearly as well pleased as her little daughter at the arrangement she had made with the Bradford children, for she hoped that their example, and the wish to keep pace with them, might help Lily to conquer her besetting fault in this instance at least; and that shame might keep her from falling behindhand with her work from week to week.

The sewing meeting being a novelty, and Lily very anxious to "see what it would be like," she was willing to be made ready in good time the next day; and actually arrived at the Bradfords' house eight minutes before three o'clock, which she, as well as the other children, took to be a decided sign of improvement in the punctuality line.

Belle was there, but not Mabel, for the latter had taken a very bad cold, and could not come out.

The little girls were soon all settled in Aunt Annie's room, each with her work; but Lily was rather dismayed, and quite ashamed, to find her mother's words proved true, and that each one of the other three children had not only commenced her work, but had completed quite a good piece upon it. Why, there was a whole seam and part of another done upon Maggie's petticoat; and she had not yet set the first stitch in hers!

"Why! haven't you done any on yours yet?" asked Bessie, in amazement. "Why didn't you begin it, Lily?"

"I thought to-day would be time enough," said Lily, rather sheepishly. "I'm sorry now I didn't begin it."

"But it's too late to be sorry now," said Bessie, gravely shaking her head. "Procrastination has been robbing Time again, Lily."

"Never mind, I'll sew very fast to-day," was Lily's answer.

As soon as she had the little girls all busy at their work, Aunt Annie took up a book, and prepared to read a story to them.

But scarcely had she commenced when the door, which stood ajar, was pushed open; and "Tootins" walked in, with an air which seemed to say she was quite sure of her welcome.

And who was "Tootins"? you will say. A kitten?

Well, I believe she was a kind of two-footed kitten; at least, she was as full of play and frolic and merry ways as any four-footed little puss that ever called old cat mother. As fond of being cuddled and petted now and then, too.

"Tootins" was the dearest, cunningest, most fascinating little two-year-old bit of mischief that ever found out she had ten fingers, and the number of uses they could be put to.

A mischief! I should think she was! Such restless, busy little fingers! "Mademoiselle Touche-à-tout" Uncle Ruthven named her. Such an inquisitive little mind! Such never-tiring, pattering little feet! Such a sweet voice, and such a crooked, cunning tongue!

When you saw her, you wanted to catch her up, and pet and hug her, she was so fair and round and dimpled; but that did not always suit Miss "Tootins." She thought her two small feet were made to be used, and she did not choose that they should be deprived of any of their privileges, except by her own free will. So she generally struggled to be put down again; and, dear me! how sorry you were to let her go!

But sometimes, as I have said, she wanted to be cuddled and petted; and then she would nestle to you, so dear and sweet, with her sunny head upon your arm, her great starry eyes fastened upon your face, while you talked baby-talk to her, or told her simple verses and stories. Understand you, do you ask? Indeed, she understood every thing you said; more than you could have believed possible.

Pure pink and white skin; eyes blue as heaven; golden hair; yes, real golden hair, for when the sunlight fell upon her curls, they looked like threads of burning gold; shoulders and hands and arms that looked as if they were only made to be kissed; a gurgling, rippling laugh; and oh, such cunning, wheedling ways! That is our "Tootins;" otherwise, Baby Annie. Our "Tootins," did I say? Well, I suppose I must call her Mrs. Bradford's "Tootins;" but then, you see, I have drawn her picture from life, and, having before my eyes just such a pet and darling of my own, it came very natural to say "our Tootins."

But how did she come by such a funny name? you will ask again.

Well, that was a name her little brother Frankie had given her when she was a tiny baby; no one knew why he did it, but he did, and he always called her by it; and of late, if any one called her by any other name, he always pretended he did not know of whom they spoke. And so "Tootins" had come to be a sort of twin pet name with "Baby," and little Annie was called as much by one as by the other.

As I have said, she came in as if quite assured of her welcome, for Baby Annie was accustomed to have her society courted, and rather imagined she was conferring a favor when she bestowed it upon her friends. Moreover, she had been promised that she should join the others on this occasion, why or with what purpose she did not understand; but she knew that her sisters had talked of Belle and Lily coming. She was fond of Belle and Lily, and had demanded a share in their company, and here they were now. This she knew very well, and so she came in, followed by old nurse, who had her own doubts as to whether baby would be considered a serviceable member of the sewing circle.

But "Tootins'" expectations proved well-founded, for she was greeted with exclamations of pleasure; and after submitting to the necessary amount of hugging and kissing, she was accommodated with a bench at Aunt Annie's feet, and mammy told that she might leave her.

But was it really possible that any one thought baby was going to sit still on that footstool? If so, she soon undeceived them; and the busy little fingers were, as usual, searching about for what mischief they could find to do.

First, she overturned Maggie's workbox, and having contrived, during the picking up of the contents, secretly to possess herself of the eyelet-piercer, was presently discovered boring holes in her own tiny shoe. The next thing which took her fancy was a small vase of flowers, which being within her reach was dragged over, the water spilled upon the floor and the flowers scattered, before Aunt Annie could prevent it. Happily, the vase was not broken, for which Miss Baby took great credit to herself, declaring over and over again that she was "dood,"—little Pharisee that she was.

By the time that this disturbance was over, order restored, and the members of the sewing society settled once more in their places, baby had retired into privacy behind the window curtain; and, being suspiciously quiet, Aunt Annie thought proper to inquire into her occupation, when she was discovered industriously taking pins from a pin-cushion, and sticking them into the carpet.

"Oh, what a mischievous, naughty little girl!" said Aunt Annie. "Shall I call mammy to take you away?"

"No, 'deed, Nan," was the answer; "Nan" being baby's name for Aunt Annie.

"Will you be good and quiet then?"

"'Es 'deed," said baby, resigning the pin-cushion into Aunt Annie's hands, and trotting off in search of fresh pastures.

A large trunk was in the room, the lid standing open; and Miss Stanton had already called baby three or four times from its dangerous neighborhood. But the straps which kept the lid from falling back seemed to have a peculiar attraction for the little one; and once more she went over to the corner where it was placed, and, taking hold of one of these straps, would in another moment have crushed both tiny hands by pulling the whole weight of the lid upon them, had not Maggie sprung up and caught it just in time.

"You had better call nurse to take her away, Maggie; she is too troublesome, and we shall accomplish nothing while she is here," said her aunt, now really vexed. But when she heard this, Baby Annie put up such a grieved lip and looked so piteous that the other children all pleaded for her; and Miss Stanton said she would try her once more.

"Shall Aunt Annie tell you a pretty story?" she asked, seating the little mischief in the corner of the sofa, where she would be out of harm's way so long as she could be persuaded to remain there.

Baby assented eagerly, for she always liked a story; and Aunt Annie began, the little one listening intently, with hands quietly folded in her lap, and her great blue eyes fixed on her aunt's face.

"Once there was a little girl, and she was a very good little girl, and always did as she was told. When her auntie said, 'You must be still,' she was as quiet as a little mouse, and made no noise. When her mamma said, 'Come here,' she always came; and when her nursey said, 'Do not touch that thing,' she never touched it. She did not take the pins, because she knew it was naughty, and that mamma would say, 'No, no;' and she did not pull at the flowers, because she knew her auntie would say, 'Let them alone;' and she did not touch Maggie's workbox, because she knew she was not to have it. And oh, dear me! why, she never would do such a naughty thing as to touch the trunk, because she knew it would hurt her little fingers, oh, so badly! and then she would have to cry. So every one loved this baby, and said, 'What a good little girl! Come here, good little girl;' and gave her pretty flowers of her own, and let her stay in the room, and did not send her away to the nursery."

Here Aunt Annie paused, to see what effect her moral tale was making on the small listener for whose benefit it was intended. Baby was intensely interested, and when Aunt Annie ceased speaking, gravely ejaculated the one syllable, "More."

The other children, who thought this extremely funny, were trying to hide their smiles that they might not spoil the lesson the story was intended to convey.

"Then there was another little girl," continued Aunt Annie, "such a naughty little girl, who would not mind what was said to her. When her mamma said, 'Don't go to the head of the stairs when the gate is open,' she would not mind, but she did go; and she fell down stairs, and bumped her poor little head. And she took the piercer, and made holes in her new shoes; and mamma said, 'Oh, the naughty baby! She must sit on the bed with no shoes on because she did such a bad thing.' And she took the scissors and cut her little fingers, and they hurt her so badly, and bled. And the pins too, and she put them in the carpet where they pricked grandmamma's feet; and grandmamma said, 'That naughty, naughty baby!' And what do you think happened to her one day? She would touch the trunk when her auntie said, 'Come away;' and the lid fell down, and cut off all the poor little fingers, and the little girl had no more fingers to play with, or to love mamma with, or to look at the pretty picture-books with. Oh, poor little girl! that was because she would not be good."

Nothing could outdo the intense gravity of the little one's face and demeanor as she listened to this thrilling tale, and drank in each word. It was certainly making a great impression, Aunt Annie thought.

"Now," she said, thinking to strengthen and give point to this, "who was the good little girl who always did as she was told?"

"Tootins," said the baby, with an air of supreme self-satisfaction, and conscious virtue, which set all the other children giggling.

"And who," asked Aunt Annie, trying to command her own face, as she put the second question, "was the naughty little girl who did all those bad things, and was so much hurt?"

"Na-a-an!" shouted baby, changing her air of delighted self-approbation to one of stern reproof and bitter indignation against her would-be teacher.

To describe the peals of gleeful laughter which followed this sudden turning of the tables would be impossible. Roguish Lily went capering and whirling about the room in an ecstasy of fun and enjoyment at this capital hit; and all thought it the most excellent joke they had heard this long time. It would have been impossible to help joining in their merry peals of laughter, even had not Aunt Annie herself been heartily amused at the little rogue's cuteness; and baby, finding she had said a good thing, joined her own rippling laugh to the general merriment, to which she further added by now saying, "Oh, dear! me so funny."

The laughter and merry voices brought mamma to see what the great joke could be; and Miss Baby now thought proper to deprive them of her society, slipping down from her nest on the sofa, and running to her mother with, —

"Me better do wis my mamma."

"Tootins" always considered she had "better" do whatever she wished to do.

And now perhaps you will say, What has all this long story about "Tootins" to do with Lily and procrastination?

Why, just this; that from the moment the baby had entered the room, Lily's attention had been entirely diverted from her sewing. In vain did that faithful little monitor, Bessie, endeavor by hints and signs, and softly whispered words, to persuade her to keep on with the work already so far behindhand. For to all her entreaties, Lily only answered, "There's time enough," or, "I'm going to do it in a minute," and so forth; while she watched the baby, and was rather disposed to encourage her in her mischief. And when Miss Stanton put little Annie up on the sofa, and began to tell her the story, Lily dropped her sewing upon the floor, and, leaving her seat, hung over the arm of the couch, listening and idling away her time. The other children were amused, too, at Annie's pranks, especially at this last one, but they kept on sewing industriously; even little Belle, who was unaccustomed to it, laboriously and with much painstaking, setting in stitch after stitch.

But even this good example had no effect on Lily; and seeing this, Aunt Annie was not sorry when "the little hindering thing" declared she had "better do wis" her mother. Mrs. Bradford thought so too; and carried away the cunning but provoking monkey.

"O Lily!" said Maggie, reproachfully, "I thought you were not going to bring Pro with you."

"Well, I didn't," said Lily. "I'm sure I've been sewing; at least, I've sewed some; and I was just looking at Annie for a moment."

"For a good many moments, Lily," said Miss Stanton; "and even when you had your work in your hand, you put in the stitches very slowly and carelessly. See there, Lily," taking up the end of the seam on which Lily was now working in great haste, in order to make up for lost time, "what long, uneven stitches, my dear child."

"Oh, they'll do, Miss Annie," said Lily. "I'll do the rest better; but I must have this seam done to-day."

Miss Stanton looked grave, and shook her head, and it was not a usual thing for gay, merry Annie Stanton to look serious; and Lily saw that she, like other people, did not think so lightly of this habit which she considered of so little consequence.

For, as you will have perceived, Lily had already forgotten the sad lesson she had received in the matter of the silver inkstand; and Maggie, Bessie, and Belle afterwards acknowledged to one another that their proverb picture had quite failed to produce the good effect they had hoped for.

"Let's keep the sewing meeting in a little longer," she said, when the hour was over, and the other children were preparing to put by their work, which had made good progress during that time.

"No," said Miss Annie, "an hour's steady work is enough for any little girl, and the others are tired. They have done enough for to-day."

"I think I'll do a little more," said Lily, who felt ashamed as she compared her own work with that of her young companions, and saw how much more they had accomplished.

"As you please," said Miss Stanton; "but I cannot attend to you longer, Lily. I am going out to dinner, and must dress now. I hope you will do better before next Thursday."

Lily went away with the others, intending to sew while they played, at least, for a while; but, as you may believe, when she saw them all engaged with their dolls, Procrastination came and put her virtuous resolution to flight, whispering that she could make up for lost time to-morrow; and, as usual, he had his way, and the petticoat was soon altogether forgotten.

VII.

WHAT CAME OF THAT.

"LILY, darling," said Mrs. Norris, on Saturday morning, "let me see how the little orphan's petticoat is coming on."

Lily went, rather sheepishly it must be confessed, and brought the skirt to her mother.

"Is this all you have done?—this little piece of a seam?" said Mrs. Norris. "And so badly too. Why, my child! what have you been thinking of? You can sew far better than this."

Lily fidgeted, and hung her head.

"Did you not all sew yesterday, when you were at Mrs. Bradford's?" asked her mamma, examining the work still more closely.

"Yes, mamma," murmured Lily.

"And did you not say Miss Annie showed you how it was to be done?"

"Yes, mamma."

"How is it, then, that you have done so very little, and that little so badly?"

"Why, you see, mamma," said Lily, hesitatingly, "I did not have much sewed, only a few stitches, and I wanted to catch up with the others; and so—and so—so the stitches wouldn't come very nice."

"And why did you not have as much accomplished as the other children? This is a very poor hour's work, dear."

"Yes, mamma; but Baby Annie was so funny, and I couldn't help looking at her, and I thought I would have time enough. It was such a horridly short hour; it was gone before I had time to do much."

"Ah, Lily," said Mrs. Norris, "it is the same old story, I fear. Procrastination, and want of attention to the duty of the time, and perhaps a little idleness and heedlessness added to them. These last two are great helpers to procrastination, Lily; or perhaps I should say, procrastination is a great helper to the sad fault of idleness. It is so very easy, when we do not feel industrious, to believe that another time will answer as well for the duty or work we should do now. So the duty is put off; and then, when shame or need calls us to the neglected task, it is hurried through heedlessly, and it may be so badly that it is quite useless, or must be done over again, as this must, my child."

"Mamma!" exclaimed Lily, in a tone in which there was displeasure as well as distress.

"Yes, indeed, my daughter. I cannot allow this to be returned to Miss Ashton with such work upon it. You are but a little girl, and no one would expect to see such neat sewing come from your hands as from those of an older person; but I should be ashamed to have it thought that my Lily cannot do better than this."

"Then I'll never have the petticoat done at all," said Lily, her eyes filling with tears. "It is 'most a week now since Miss Ashton gave them to us, and if I have to take that out it will be all to do from the beginning, and Maggie and Bessie and Belle have ever so much done on theirs, and I shan't have one stitch done on mine."

Mrs. Norris looked grieved at the rebellious tone.

"Whose fault is it, Lily?" she asked sorrowfully.

Lily hesitated for a moment; then, for the first time in her life, temper had the better of her love and reverence for her mother, and she answered passionately, —

"Yours, if you make me pull that out!"

For a moment, surprise held Mrs. Norris silent and motionless. Never before had Lily spoken so to her; never before had she been other than her loving, docile little child, not always strictly obedient it might be, but that was not so much from wilfulness as from that sad habit of putting off, — of not obeying at once.

Then the surprise died out, and left only pain and grief; and while Lily was wondering what mamma would do, could do, after such a dreadful thing as that (for the very utterance of the words had sobered her, and calmed down her temper), Mrs. Norris rose, and laying down the skirt, without one word, without one look at her naughty little child, slowly and sorrowfully left the room.

Lily stood still one moment, herself almost breathless with surprise and dismay at what she had done. Had she really said such dreadful words to mamma? and could mamma ever, ever forgive them? Her own dear, loving, indulgent mamma to hear such words from the lips of her own, only little daughter. What would papa say, what would Tom say, when they should know it? what would Maggie and Bessie say? For when mamma treated her as she deserved to be treated from this time forth, they would surely know that something was wrong, and must learn what she had done. And, oh! how angry God must be with her!

Some little boys and girls, who are in the habit of saying unkind and disrespectful things to their mothers, — and, alas! there are too many such, — may wonder at our Lily's distress and remorse; but Lily was not accustomed to behave in this way to her mother; as you have heard, it was the first time in her life that she had done so, and now she was fairly frightened when she remembered how she had let passion master her.

And what had brought this about?

Lily did not think of it just then, in all the tumult of feeling which swelled her little heart; but had it not all arisen from the sad habit of procrastination, of which she thought so lightly?

She felt as if she dared not run after her mother, and ask her forgiveness. True, mamma always was ready to forgive her when she was penitent after any naughtiness; but then—oh! she had never, never done any thing like this before—and Lily threw herself down upon the rug in a paroxysm of tears and sobs.

By and by the door was opened, and Tom came in. He stood still for a moment in surprise at the state in which he found his little sister, then came forward.

"My pet, what is it? What is the matter?" he said, stooping over her, and trying to raise her. But Lily resisted; and so Tom sat down on the floor beside her. A fresh burst of sobs came from Lily.

"What is it, dear?" asked Tom again. "Shall I call mamma?"

"Oh, no, no!" sobbed Lily. "She wouldn't c-c-come if you did. She'll never want to come near m-me a-a-gain."

"Why? What is wrong?" asked Tom, whose fears that Lily was ill or had hurt herself were now removed; for he saw that it was not bodily but mental trouble which ailed her.

"Oh! I've done the most horrid, the most dreadful thing, Tom," confessed Lily, still hardly able to speak for the fast-coming tears and sobs. "Oh! I spoke so wickedly to mamma; to my own dear, precious, darling mamma. It was 'most worse than the inkstand, oh, it was, it was! I'm so bad, oh, such a bad child!"

"Are you willing to tell me about it?" asked Tom, soothingly.

Lily raised her head, and threw it upon her brother's knee, allowing him to wipe away her tears; although, as she told her story, they flowed as fast as he dried them.

"Lily," said Tom, hoping that this might prove a good lesson to her,—ah! how often had Lily's friends vainly hoped that the trouble she brought upon herself might prove of service to her,—"Lily, how was it that your work was so very badly done?"

And Lily made a fresh confession, Tom gently leading her back to what he truly suspected to be the first cause of all this difficulty.

"Lily, dear," he said, "I am sure I do not want to seem to find fault with you, or to reproach you when you are feeling so badly; but I would like you to see how all this has come about. You think it such a small fault, such a very little thing, to put off your duties, and even your pleasures, if it happens to suit the convenience of the moment. As to pleasures, I suppose that does not matter much, so long as we do not let our want of punctuality interfere with the pleasure of others; but although it may not be what we call a great sin in itself, just see into what sin and sorrow procrastination may lead us. One little duty neglected or put off may interfere with another; or, as you have done, we may have to hurry through with it in such a manner as to leave it worse than if we had not tried to do it at all. And so we are disappointed and vexed, and perhaps we grow cross and ill-tempered, or fly into a passion, and do some very wrong or unkind thing."

"Yes; or behave worse than any child that ever lived, to our darling, lovely, precious mammas, just like me," broke forth poor, penitent Lily.

"Yes," said Tom, gravely, but kindly, "you see to what it has led you,—disrespect and impertinence to dear mamma. Is not this enough, Lil darling, to show you how much pain and trouble may come from this habit, and why you ought to try to break yourself of it? It is not only the inconvenience which must come from it, but the wrong which may grow from it, which should teach us to try and keep it from gaining a hold upon us. Do you see, Lil?"

"I should think I did," said Lily, dolefully, though she now sat upright, but with a most rueful and despairing countenance. "I should think it had made me bad enough to see what it can do. But, Tom,"—with an admiring look at her brother from the midst of her gloom and distress,—"but, Tom, what a wise boy you are! You talk as if you were grown up; quite as if you were a minister; only I understand all you say, and I don't understand all ministers say."

"No, I suppose not," said Tom, speaking more gayly; "but we will not have any more preaching just now, only—I would like to tell you a story, Lily. Shall I?"

"Yes, indeed, please do," answered Lily, brightening a little at the prospect.

"It is a very sad story, but I thought it would just fit here," said her brother.

"I'm not in a state of mind for a pleasant story," said Lily, who had lately fallen into the way of using long words, and "grown-up" phrases, after the example of her little friends, Maggie and Bessie.

"No, I suppose not," said Tom, suppressing all inclination to smile. "Well, you know Will Sturges, Lily?"

"Oh, yes, that very sorry-looking boy, whose father is dead, you told me," said Lily. "Tom, it always makes me feel sorry to see him. He hardly ever smiles, or looks happy. You know mamma told you to ask him here often, and see if you could not brighten him up; but he don't seem to brighten up at all. Bessie said he looked 'as if he had a weight on his mind' all the time."

"Ah! that is just it," said Tom. "He has a terrible weight on his mind; a grief that is there night and day. He thinks it is through his fault that his father was killed; and I suppose that it is so. At least it was brought about by a small neglect of his, — procrastination, or putting off, Lily."

"Did he ever put off?" asked the little girl, opening great eyes of wonder. "Why, he always seems so very punctual, so very ready just when he ought to be."

"Yes," said Tom, "but he was not always so, dear. Never was a more unpunctual, a more dilatory boy than Will Sturges used to be. Poor dear fellow! he has learned better by such a sad lesson. I hope my little sister may never have the like."

"I'm sure," said Lily, "I don't know who has had a sad lesson, if I have not."

"Ah! but, Lily," said her brother, "you have yet the time and chance to show you are sorry, and want to try to do better — if you really do repent — and to gain forgiveness from the one you have injured, — dear mamma; but poor Will, he never had the chance to make up for his neglect of his duty."

"Tell me," begged Lily, all curiosity and interest.

"Well," said Tom, "Will Sturges used to be, as he is now, about the brightest and quickest boy in our class."

Lily shook her head doubtfully at this; it was all Tom's modesty, she thought, and more than she could conveniently believe. Tom understood her, but continued his story without interruption.

"But, for all that, he never was at the head of his class, nor even took a very high standing in it; for never was such a boy for being behindhand as Will Sturges. Every thing that could be put off was put off, and he never seemed to like to attend to any duty or task at the proper moment. It was not laziness either, for he would leave some small task which should have been done at once, perhaps to take up one that was far harder, but which might well have waited till he had finished the first. He never could be persuaded to attend to his regular lessons first, but would let himself be led away from them, not always by play or pleasure, but often to take up some book which there was no need for him to study, always believing and saying that there was 'time enough' — 'no hurry' — 'by and by he would do it,' and so forth; until, as you may suppose, his lessons were left until the last moment, when they would be scrambled through, and Will just contrived to keep himself from disgrace. It was so with every thing; he never was ready in time for either work or pleasure. If he were going on a journey, or any excursion, ten to one but he was left behind by being too late for the boat or train; all his own fault too, for his father and mother used to take pains enough to have him ready in time. When Mr. Peters took the school on a picnic or frolic, it was always a part of the entertainment to see Will come tearing down the dock, or by the side of the cars just at the last moment, often after the last moment, and when it was too late. No boy in school had so many tardy marks; none lost so many books, papers, and pencils, because he always thought it was time enough to put them in their places by and by. No lesson did him any good, no disappointment or inconvenience he brought upon himself seemed to cure him; until at last the sad thing happened of which I am going to tell you.

"One afternoon his father said to him, 'Will, if you are going out, I wish these papers posted at the station. Take them with you, and attend to them at once, my son, before you go upon your own errand. They must go to grandfather by to-night's train. Can I depend upon you for once?' 'Yes, indeed, you may, sir,' promised Will, meaning what he said too; and when he left the house, he intended to go directly to the post-office station. But he had not gone far when he met a friend; and this boy begged him to go home with him, and see a fine new dog he had just bought. Will hesitated, looked at his watch, and found that there were still nearly two hours before the next mail would leave the station, that mail by which the papers must go if they were to reach the evening train. 'There'll be plenty of time, and all papa cared for was that they should reach the station before the mail left it,' he said to himself; and he went with his friend. He stayed with him more than an hour; then he said good-by, having, as he promised himself, more than time enough to reach the post, and mail his papers. But, just as he was about leaving the house, a little brother of his friend fell downstairs, hurting himself very badly; and, in the hurry and distress of the moment, he was begged to run for the doctor. He forgot his papers — indeed, how could one refuse such an errand at such a time? — and ran for the doctor, who lived far off, and in quite a different direction from the station. This last was not his fault, and if he had obeyed his father at once all would have been right; but, what with one thing and another, he was too late, and the mail had left. He tried all he could to send the papers by that evening train, but it was useless, for he could find no one to take charge of them, and he knew it would not do to trust them to chance hands. So he could do nothing but take them home again, which he did, and confessed his fault. His father looked very grave; but, as poor Will has often told me, did not scold him, only saying, 'Then I shall probably have to leave town myself to-morrow, and it will be a great inconvenience to me. I fear, my boy, that you will never learn the value of punctuality and the evil of procrastination until they are taught you by some severe lesson.' Poor, dear old Will! what a lesson that was to be! Well, his father was telegraphed the next day to come himself, since the papers had not arrived; and he left his home, Lily, never to come back. The train by which he went met with a fearful accident, and Mr. Sturges was killed in an instant. And from that day Will has been the sad, melancholy fellow you see him; for he blames himself for his father's death, and says but for him he would have remained at home, and so been safe. And, Lily, we must see that it is so, and that, if Will had not put off the duty he should have attended to, all this would probably never have taken place. If you could hear him talk about it!"

Lily drew a long sigh, partly from pity for Will Sturges, partly from dread of what sorrows might come to herself if she were not cured of this sad fault, then said, —

"But, after all, Tom, he was not so bad to his father as I was to mamma, for he did not mean to be naughty, and I'm afraid I did. Do you know, I was in a real passion, a passionate passion, with mamma. O, Tom! what shall I do?"

"What ought you to do first?" asked Tom.

"Go and ask mamma to forgive me; but how can she, Tom?" asked Lily, sobbing again.

"Mamma would forgive any thing, if she thought you were truly sorry," said her brother.

"I'm sure I am," answered the little girl. "If she could see in my heart, she would know it very well."

"You can show her what is in your heart, dear, by letting her see that you are really trying to break yourself of the troublesome fault which has led you to behave so to her."

Lily threw her arms around her brother's neck, and kissed him; the next moment she was gone in search of her mamma. When she reached her, she could find no words, none but a piteous "O mamma!" But her voice and her face spoke for her; and in another moment she was clinging fast around her mother's neck, her dear, kind arms about her, her kiss of forgiveness on the little head which buried itself in shame and contrition upon her shoulder.

But, though Lily was forgiven, she could not recover her spirits all that day, a thing very unusual with her; but then, as she said, she had "never been so wickedly naughty before," and she felt as if she could not do enough to make up to her mother for her offence.

She was rather droll, too, as she was apt to be, when by any means she fell into low spirits.

When her papa came home, she did not go to meet him with her usual light and dancing step; and he missed that, and the joyous face with which she was accustomed to greet him.

"Why," he said, "what ails my little sunbeam to-day?" for Mr. Norris had heard of Belle's idea about the sunbeams in the family, and he delighted to call his Lily so.

"I'm not a sunbeam to-day, papa," said Lily.

"You're not a little cloud, I hope," said papa.

"Oh, no!" answered Lily, mournfully, "not even so good as a cloud. I've been so very, very naughty that I believe I'm a—a"—Lily was racking her imagination for a comparison that should seem severe enough enough—"I've been quite a January thaw, papa."

Mr. Norris opened the door of the coat closet, and hastily put his head therein, taking a remarkably long time to hang up his hat, Lily thought.

Now you must know that a January thaw was Lily's idea of all that was most disagreeable in the weather. For, the last winter, she had had a severe attack of diphtheria; and just as she was well enough to go out, a long spell of damp, foggy days set in, keeping her a prisoner for some weeks longer, and depriving her of many little pleasures on which she had set her heart.

"She must not go outside of the door until this January thaw is over," the doctor said several times; and Lily had come to look upon this as the very worst specimen of weather.

"Don't you scorn me, papa?" she asked, when she had made her confession to him.

"No, I do not scorn you by any means, Lily," he answered; "and I am glad to see that you do really feel your fault, for it gives me hope that you may try to correct it with more earnestness than you have yet done."

And then he talked to her for some time longer, setting before her very plainly all the trouble and inconvenience, yes, and sin too, which might come from indulgence in this habit of procrastination.

Certainly our Lily did not want for teachers, both wise and kind; for her friends, young and old, seemed all to have set themselves to give her help in the right way, if she would but heed them.

<h1 style="text-align:center">VIII.</h1>

<h2 style="text-align:center">A LITTLE TALK.</h2>

IT did really seem now that Lily was taking herself to task in earnest, and it was surprising to see how much she improved during the next few days. There was no more dilly-dallying with any little duty or task she had to perform; if her mother or any other person asked some small service from her, she ran promptly and at once; when Nora called her to make ready for school or her walk, there was no more stopping "only to do this," or "just to look at that." She was not once tardy at school; not once late at meals, a thing which her father disliked extremely, but to which Lily had until now paid but little heed. Play and nonsense were given up at school, save at the proper times, and she came to her classes with her lessons correctly prepared; for, when Lily failed here, it was not from stupidity, or want of quickness, but simply from idleness, or her habit of saying "there's time enough still."

The little petticoat, too, was progressing nicely, with a prospect of being finished in time after all; for Lily had begged her mamma to divide it off into certain portions, so much to be done on each day, that she might know her appointed task, and so be sure to have it completed. And she persevered, though the little unaccustomed fingers did grow rather tired every day before they were through with the allotted portion of seam or hem; for, having been so idle, or rather procrastinating, she found it hard to make up for lost time. Now she regretted that she had not taken the advice of her mother and teacher, and chosen one of the little aprons, instead of the petticoat.

Nora could not bear to see her plodding away over it, and more than once begged Mrs. Norris to let her help Lily, or "give her a lift," as she called it.

But Mrs. Norris refused, for she had told Lily that she would not allow this; and much as she would have liked to relieve her little girl, she did not think it best, and hoped that the burden she had brought upon herself might be of service to her.

However, when the next Thursday came, and Lily was to go to the second "sewing meeting," she was very glad that she had so much done on her petticoat.

"For I would be too ashamed to go to-day if I had not done better than I did last week, mamma," she said. "And two or three of the children in our class have finished their work already; and here is old me with mine not quite half done."

Lily was very "scornful," as she would have called it, of herself in these days, and rather delighted in heaping uncomplimentary names and reproaches upon her own head.

When she reached Mrs. Bradford's house at the appointed time, she was rather dismayed to find that, in spite of her industry of the last few days, the other children had accomplished much more than she had done. Maggie's skirt was so near completion that she had but a little piece of the hem to do; and she had only left this, in order that she might, as she said keep company with the rest in the sewing meeting. And Maggie had made a button-hole! Yes, actually made a button-hole! It was her first attempt, but still it was tolerably well done. It had cost her a good deal of trouble too, and even some few tears; but she had persevered, and now was glad that she had done so.

"Patience and Perseverance conquer all things, you know," she said to Lily, when Bessie, with some pardonable pride in her sister's success, displayed this triumph of art; "but I really thought that button-hole must conquer me, only I wouldn't let it, if I did cry a little about it."

Bessie, too, had nearly finished her bag; and though Belle was rather behind the others, she had a fair prospect of being quite through with her task in time.

They all encouraged Lily, and told her she might still finish her petticoat by the appointed day, if she would but continue to do as well as she was now doing.

The sewing meeting passed off this day without hindrance; for Baby Annie was not admitted; and there was nothing else especially to take off Lily's attention from the task in hand. Aunt Annie read an interesting story, it was true, but all the little girls sewed industriously as they listened; and at the end of the hour Maggie's petticoat and Bessie's bag were completed, while those of Belle and Lily had made fair progress.

"I have only three more days," said the latter, "for you know we have to give in the things on Tuesday, and this is Thursday."

Lily's tone was rather hopeless.

"I think you might finish your skirt in two days, Lily," said Miss Stanton. "Two hours' steady work such as you have given to it to-day would be quite time enough. If I were you I should sew one hour to-morrow, and one on Saturday, so that you may have little or nothing for your last day, Monday."

"Why wouldn't it do just as well to keep some for Monday?" asked Lily, folding up her work.

"Only that if you could finish it in the next two days it would be better," answered Miss Annie, "because something might happen to prevent you from doing so at the last moment."

"Don't have any more putting-off fits, Lily," said Maggie. "Don't you find 'distance lends enchantment to the view' of Pro? What are you laughing at, Aunt Annie? There is such a proverb, for I read it this very morning, only I didn't think I should have a good chance to use it so soon. I'll show it to you, so you need not think I made it up."

"Yes, I know," said Annie, catching the rosy, eager face between her two hands, and lovingly kissing either dimpled cheek. "It is an old, old proverb, and one very well known, dear Maggie; and let us hope that Procrastination may indeed look so much better at a distance than near at hand that Lily may keep it there, and not let it come near her."

"Aunt Annie," said Bessie, "you must be a very laughable person, for so often you laugh at things that we don't think funny at all."

"That is true," answered Aunt Annie, whose eyes were brimming with mischief, while she laughed more merrily than ever.

"Well," said Lily, "I did not quite understand what Maggie meant till Miss Annie said that, but I do know now; and, indeed, I do think Pro is better far off than close by. I'm sure I am a great deal better anyway, and I shall never let him come near me again."

Bessie stood looking gravely at her as she spoke.

"I see you don't quite trust me, Bessie," said Lily, "but you'll see. If you only knew all that I know, you'd learn what good reason I have for believing I shall never procrastinate again; but I'd rather not tell you what it is."

For Lily did really shrink from letting her little playmates know of her sad behavior to her dear mother, although she could not refrain from alluding to it in this mysterious manner.

"You know you're all coming to my house to spend the day with me on Saturday," she continued; "and before you come, I shall have the petticoat all finished, and will show it to you."

Lily kept faithfully to her resolution upon the next day, sewing industriously for a full hour, and then putting by her work with the consciousness that she had accomplished all that could be expected of her for that day. Perhaps she had been further encouraged to do so by hearing most of her young schoolmates say that morning that their little garments were quite finished, and ready to be handed in to Miss Ashton on Tuesday. Even Mabel Walton, although she had been quite ill with a bad cold, had completed her bag; and little Belle hoped and expected to put the last stitches in her's on that afternoon.

"Is your apron done, Nellie?" asked Lily of Nellie Ransom.

"Not quite," answered Nellie, "and I shall not finish it before to-morrow, for my two little cousins are in town to-day, and I must give up this afternoon to them. I am glad that I took the apron instead of the petticoat, for I am sure I should not have had time to make the last."

"You could have tried," said Gracie. "I'm sure a petticoat is not so much to make. Mine was all done on Saturday evening, and I did not have any help or showing either. Mamma is away, and I wouldn't let my nurse help me, but did it every bit myself. But then every one says I'm uncommonly handy with my needle;" and Gracie gave her head the toss which always excited the displeasure of her schoolmates.

"Well," said Nellie, coloring and hesitating a little, "I felt pretty sure that I could not make the petticoat in time, and I thought it was better to take that which I knew I could do; and now you see I should feel badly if I could not bring in my work when the rest do."

"Yes, and you were very right," said Belle. "I told Aunt Margaret about you, and she said you were a wise, prudent little girl."

"I wouldn't be such a slow poke as Nellie, would you?" whispered Gracie to Lily, when Nellie had moved away a little.

"I s'pose I'd be as I was made, and I s'pose you'd be as you were made," said Lily, loftily, for her "scorn," as she would have called it, was always excited by Gracie's attempts to exalt herself above her companions and schoolmates, and it rather delighted her to put Gracie down.

This was difficult, however. Gracie's self-sufficiency was so great that only a very hard blow could overthrow it, even for a moment; and Lily was too much afraid of being considered an anti-politer to speak her mind as plainly as she might otherwise have done.

So Gracie was not at all rebuffed by the answer she received; and, so far from taking it as the reproof Lily intended it to be, only replied, —

"Yes, of course; but I'm very glad I was made smarter than Nellie. Why, sometimes I can learn three lessons while she is learning one, she is so slow and stupid!"

"She is not stupid," retorted Lily, forgetting her determination to "be courteous" in her indignation; and, indeed, Gracie often made it difficult for those about her to keep to this resolution. "She is not stupid, and if she is a little bit slow about learning, she always knows her lessons perfectly, and never misses; no, never. You know she's been head of the spelling class for most a year; you know it, Gracie, and Miss Ashton says she is one of her very best scholars. And the whole world knows" — Lily was waxing energetic in her defence, and more earnest to be emphatic than strictly according to facts — "the whole world knows that she writes the best compositions in our class since Maggie Bradford left."

"Pooh! I never thought Maggie's compositions were so very great," said Gracie.

"That shows you're no judge, and have very little common sense," said Lily severely. "I'm sure no one could write better poetry than that poem she wrote for me, and you might be proud if you could make such lovely verses. But I don't want to quarrel with you, Gracie, so we'd better not talk any more about it, 'cause I do feel like saying something not courteous to you."

Gracie in her turn would have liked to say something that was not very pleasant, but she felt that she could not well do so when Lily declared her intention of not quarrelling, and retired in such a graceful manner from the threatened dispute. Still she did feel that somehow Lily had had the best of it, and had rather taken her down, as she was apt to do when Gracie displayed her vanity and self-conceit.

Moreover, clever and bright though she might be at her lessons, Gracie was not very quick at words; and she often felt that Lily had the advantage of her in their too frequent little disputes. And now while she was hesitating as to whether she should make a sharp answer, and what that answer should be, Miss Ashton came in and rang the bell; so that the opportunity, or I should say temptation, for further contention was at an end.

"I hope," said Miss Ashton, when the time came for dismissing school, "I hope that not one of my little girls will fail me on Tuesday. I should be very much disappointed, and mortified too, if I did not receive each garment quite finished and ready for use. Some of you I know are already through with the work which you have undertaken; and after what I have said, I believe and hope there is no one who will be willing to bring hers unfinished."

Her eye rested on Lily as she spoke. Perhaps she was hardly conscious that it was so, but she almost involuntarily turned to her as the one who was most likely to fail; and, however that might be, the little girl felt herself called upon to answer, not only for herself, but for the whole class.

"We'll be very sure to be ready, Miss Ashton," she said; "and I will too. I see you are afraid of me, but you need not be, for I b'lieve I'm quite cured now of putting off."

Miss Ashton smiled, but it was rather a doubtful smile, for she feared that Lily was too confident of herself, and the strength of her own resolutions.

So, as I have said, all this made Lily feel very industrious and prompt that day; and as soon as she was at liberty for the work, she set to her task at once, and accomplished it without delay.

But notwithstanding this, the day did not pass by without a fall into the old bad habit, as you shall learn.

IX.

SATURDAY MORNING'S WORK.

SATURDAY came, a bright and beautiful day, as Lily rejoiced to see when she ran to the window and peeped out as soon as she was out of her little bed.

For she was to have quite a party of children to spend the day with her, and she had been very anxious that the weather should be pleasant.

Maggie and Bessie, Belle and Mabel, and Nellie and Carrie Ransom were all coming, and they expected to have a great frolic. All Lily's playmates were fond of visiting her, not only because they loved her, and her home was a pleasant one, but also because there was such a grand play-room in Mr. Norris' house.

This was a great open attic hall or gallery. The house was a large one, and this open space ran across the whole width of it, the attic rooms being at either end, and a staircase coming up at the side. But this was shut in by a door at the foot of the flight, so that it was quite secluded, and considered rather an advantage, as it afforded a kind of retiring room. There were large bins ranged on the opposite side from the stairs, which had once been used to hold coal and wood; but they were empty now, and the top of the lids afforded capital seats for the spectators who witnessed certain performances which frequently took place in the open arena. Never was there such a famous garret, or one which had seen greater sport and fun.

Here the children could make as much noise as they pleased without fear of disturbing older people; here there was plenty of space for playing "tag," "hunt the slipper," "chairs," or any other frolicsome game; here they acted proverbs, charades, and so forth. These last were now their favorite amusements, and Mr. Norris' attic was considered the best place for their performance.

For, added to these other advantages, there was also a room devoted to the storing of all manner of odds and ends which were not in general use, and were stored there to be out of the way; and with certain of these articles the children were allowed to do as they pleased, and to make them serviceable in their games and plays. Among them were two or three old trunks full of old party dresses and ribbons; and any little girl can imagine what delightful means these afforded for "dressing up." There were flags, too, of various sizes and conditions, old-fashioned curtain fixtures, and even a tent of striped red and white canvas. All these Lily and her playmates were allowed to convert to their own uses, so long as they destroyed nothing; and many an hour did patient Nora, ever devoted to the pleasure of her nursling, spend in putting them to rights after they had been thoroughly rummaged and scattered abroad.

Chief among the treasures in the attic was an old rocking-horse which had belonged to Tom; at least he had once been a rocking-horse, but he had now not only lost his

60

rockers, but also his hind legs. Strange to say, however, this did not at all interfere with his usefulness; perhaps it rather added to it, for when he was supposed to fill his original character, namely, that of a horse, he was accommodated with two imaginary limbs in the place of the missing members, and he never complained that they did not answer the purpose quite as well.

The number of uses to which he was put, and the characters he was supposed to represent, would be impossible to tell. Sometimes he was a prince, and sometimes a beggar or a robber; sometimes a servant, and sometimes a lover or husband; sometimes a little boy, at others a cross old man; again he was converted into an elephant by having the end of a curved iron pipe thrust into his mouth, or into a camel by a pillow upon his back; at times, a fierce wild beast, growling and raging; at others, the meekest of sheep or cows, mild and gentle in all respects. At one time he spoke in a squeaking but plaintive voice; at another in what was supposed to be a deep, roaring bass.

I forgot to say that he had lost his tail as well as his legs; and his beauty was farther increased by the fact that Maggie and Lily, finding his ears inconvenient for the proper fitting of crowns, caps, wreaths, and other decorations, had cropped them close to his head. He had also been shorn of his hair in various places, which gave him a mangy and distressed appearance; so that, save in the eyes of his most intimate and attached friends, he was not a horse of very fine personal appearance.

This gallant and accommodating steed rejoiced in the name of Sir Percy Hotspur; but this was laid aside when convenience demanded it, and he obligingly answered to the name of the moment.

Dear to the hearts of Lily and her young friends was Sir Percy Hotspur; and he was always tenderly cared for after he was through with his performances, being left to repose in the intervals in a corner of the attic, with his head upon an old sofa pillow, and carefully covered with a disused carriage robe.

What a long history of an old rocking-horse, you may say, and so it is; but, you see, Sir Percy Hotspur played a very important part in Lily's life, and she was deeply attached to him, and as this is her story, whatever concerned her deserves our attention.

With so many attractions, you may believe that an invitation to Lily's house was always considered desirable, and eagerly accepted.

Never, I think, were four little girls who found more enjoyment in their small lives and in one another, than our Maggie and Bessie, Belle and Lily. They were so much together that whatever interested one interested all the others, and any pleasure was increased if they could all share it together.

But we must go to the history of this Saturday.

"Lily," said Mrs. Norris, as the family left the breakfast table, "it is nine o'clock now; and if I were you, I would finish that little petticoat at once. I think you can do it in an hour, and then it will be off your mind and conscience; and after you have practised for half an hour, you can enjoy yourself for the rest of the day as you please."

"I don't believe the children will come before twelve o'clock, do you, mamma?" asked Lily.

"No, probably not."

"Then I have three hours," said Lily. "That is lots of time, and I shall be sure to have it done, even if I don't begin right away."

"Take care, Lily," said her mother, lifting a warning finger, and shaking her head with a smile which told the little girl what that warning meant.

"Don't be afraid, mamma," she answered "I'll be sure to do it this morning; and even if I did not quite finish it, I have Monday too."

Again Mrs. Norris shook her head, and this time without the smile; for she plainly saw that Lily was in one of her careless, putting off moods, and she feared the work would suffer.

"I am going right away, mamma," said Lily, as she saw how grave her mother looked; and away she danced, singing as she went.

But as she ran through the hall, she met her brother Tom with his puppy, which he was going to take for a walk. Lily never saw the little dog without stopping to have a romp with him, and the playful little fellow was growing fond of her already, and was always eager for the frolic with which she indulged him.

He sprang upon her now, whining and crying with pleasure at seeing her, and Lily stopped, of course, to pet him, and then began racing up and down through the hall; while Tom good-naturedly waited, and stood by, laughing at the antics of the two frolicsome young things. Gay and careless as the puppy himself, Lily had no more thought for the task awaiting her.

I do not know that she should be very much blamed for this; but few little girls who would not have done the same, and Lily knew that there was much more than time enough for the completion of the petticoat. But I want to show you how the moments, yes, and the hours too, slipped away; how little bits of idling and procrastination stole away the time before she was aware, and in the end brought her into sad trouble.

A quarter of an hour went by in Lily's frolic with the puppy, until at last Tom said he must go.

"I would take you with me, Lil," he said, "only that I know mamma wishes you to do your work."

"Yes," said Lily reluctantly; and but for very shame she would have begged to put off her work and accompany him.

Tom and his dog were gone, and Lily sauntered towards the sitting-room.

"I don't feel a bit like sewing now," she said to herself. "I could have gone with Tom, and been back time enough to finish my petticoat. Every one is so particular about my putting-off, and they never want me to do any thing I want to. But I s'pose I'll have to finish the old thing now."

Lily, you see, was allowing temptation to creep in. She did not still its first whisperings, but suffered them to make her feel discontented and fretful.

She had stopped at the foot of the staircase, and with both hands clasped about the newel-post, was swaying herself back and forth, when Nora spoke to her from the head of the stairs.

"Miss Lily," she said, by way of a gentle reminder, "do you need any help with your work?"

"No, I b'lieve not," answered the little girl. "If I do, I'll come to you. I was just thinking where I'd go to sew."

"Will you come to the nursery? It is all put in order," asked Nora, anxious to carry her point, and seeing from Lily's manner that her old enemy was busy with her.

"I'll see presently," said Lily. "I'm just going to the little parlor to look for my petticoat. I forget what I did with it yesterday when I had done sewing."

And, leaving her hold of the banisters, she crossed the hall. But as she passed the open door of the drawing-room, the piano caught her eye, and turned her thoughts into another channel.

"I think I'll go and practise first," she said. "It's all the same thing, and I can do the petticoat afterwards. I have just the same time."

This was true enough, but Lily was not wise, for she liked to practise, and she did not like to sew; and it would have been better for her to have done with the least pleasant duty first.

She placed herself at the piano, and, I must do her the justice to say, practised steadily for half an hour.

"It is ten minutes of ten," she said, looking at the clock. "Oh, there's lots of time yet; I can stay here a little longer. I'm going to practise this new piece some more."

This new piece was one Miss Ashton had given her the day before, so that she had had but one lesson on it; and it had all the charm of novelty to her, besides being, as she thought, the prettiest piece she had ever played.

"I'll astonish Miss Ashton by letting her see how well I have learned it," she said to herself; and she remained at the piano, playing over and over again the lively little waltz, until her mother's voice at the door recalled her to her neglected duty.

"Lily," it said, "you have been practising more than half an hour, dear."

"Yes, mamma," said Lily, glancing over at the clock again; "more than three quarters; but my new music is so very pretty, and I want Miss Ashton to be quite surprised with my knowing it so well."

"I am afraid Miss Ashton may have a less agreeable surprise if you do not take care, my darling," said Mrs. Norris gravely.

"Oh, you mean about the petticoat, mamma; but there's lots and lots of time. I b'lieve Pro has had hold of me this morning," said Lily, jumping down from the piano stool, "and I'll come right away; but you see I was so very sure about having time enough to-day, mamma, that it did not make so much difference. There's a good deal of time yet to-day, and I have Monday too."

"Put away your music, Lily," said her mother; and she stood waiting while Lily laid in its place the music she would have left scattered over the piano. Perhaps Mrs. Norris thought it just as well not to lose sight again of her heedless little daughter until she had her settled at her work.

"Bring your work-box to my room," said Mrs. Norris. "I have something to do there, and we will have a nice, cosey time."

Lily ran for the box, and was back with it in a moment, for as she went she said to herself, —

"I b'lieve I've let Pro steal a good many little thefts already this morning; now I'll just send him off right away. I have plenty of time yet, but now I really must make haste."

Lily's work-box was of rather formidable dimensions; indeed, some people thought it but one stage removed from a small trunk. It had been presented to her by an old lady with whom she was a great pet, and although it was extremely inconvenient in regard to size and weight, it was very handsomely fitted up with mother-of-pearl and silver, and contained every implement which could be needed by the most accomplished needle-woman. Upon the lid was a silver plate, with "For an industrious little girl" engraved upon it.

Now as we know, our Lily was by no means an industrious little girl; nevertheless she took great pride and delight in this "ark," as Tom privately called it; and, although she had two or three other work-boxes and baskets much more suitable and convenient in point of size, she made use of this one whenever she could do so.

"It held so much," she said, and indeed it did; and here the petticoat had reposed in the intervals when she was not busy with it; that is, when Lily had put it away in a proper manner.

She followed her mother with this ponderous treasure clasped in both arms; and, when she reached mamma's room, brought her little chair, and opened the box.

"Why," she said, when she had removed the upper tray which held all the dainty implements, and looked into the empty space beneath, "why, where is my petticoat? Somebody has gone and taken it out. Mamma, did you take it?"

"No, dear, I have not touched it," said Mrs. Norris. "Did you put it away yesterday?"

"Yes, mamma, you know I always put it in here. I'll ask Nora;" and away ran Lily to the nursery.

"Nora, did you take my orphan petticoat out of my work-box?" she asked.

"No, indeed, dear; and why would I touch it, unless you wanted some help with it?" answered Nora.

Back went Lily to her mamma's room, troubled and indignant.

"Mamma, some one has taken it. I never knew any thing so mean. Nora don't know any thing about it."

"Who would take it, Lily? I certainly did not, and you say Nora did not. Papa or Tom could have no reason for touching it. I will tell you what I think."

"What mamma?" asked Lily, anxiously.

"That you could not have put it away yesterday when you stopped sewing upon it. Think a moment, my daughter; can you distinctly recollect putting it away in your box?"

Lily stood considering one moment; then dismay and shame gradually overspread her face.

"No, mamma, I just believe I did not. When I was going to put away my petticoat in the box, I heard papa come in, and I wanted to know why he had come home so early; so I thought I would just wait one moment, and put it away when I had asked him, and I dropped it on the floor and ran to papa. And you know he had come to take us to see those pictures, and I never thought another thing about the petticoat. I quite forgot I had not put it away when I told you I had. I will go and look in the sitting-room where I was sewing yesterday."

But her search proved fruitless, although she certainly did look thoroughly through every part of the room. Nora was called, and took her part, but all in vain; and at last mamma came. Mrs. Norris rather felt that she should let Lily be at all the trouble of finding the petticoat for herself; but the child seemed so grieved that she could not bear to punish her in that way. But mamma was not more successful than her little daughter and the nurse had been, although in the end every servant was questioned, and every room searched.

"It is very strange. Are you quite sure you have not seen it, Hannah?" asked Mrs. Norris of her chambermaid, a rather dull girl, who had been but a short time in the house. "Have you seen nothing of the kind lying about in the sitting-room, or did you not touch Miss Lily's box?"

"Miss Lily's harnsum box, is it, ma'am? Sure, and I did see that a sittin' on the floor, where I thought you'd not be plased to see it at all at all, so I just lifted it to the table where I seen it sittin' before; but ne'er a thing I seen beside it. It wouldn't be Miss Lily's work what I found the puppy a pullin' round the ary, ma'am,—the mischavous baste that he is, my heart's most broke with him,—an' I didn't take heed what it was, but seein' it that dirty, I just put it in the basket with the siled clothes."

Away went Lily, Nora after her; and, sure enough, the latter soon fished out the unfortunate little petticoat from the soiled-clothes basket. Now, indeed, Lily was distressed, and cried bitterly, for the thing was in no state to be touched until it had been washed. It was easy to imagine how it had happened. The puppy, who was growing very mischievous, and who, like many another young thing, was fond of a forbidden plaything, had probably found the petticoat lying where Lily had heedlessly dropped it upon the floor; and, watching his opportunity, had dragged it from the room, down stairs, and out into the back area, where Hannah had rescued it, happily before it was torn and chewed to bits, but not before it was sadly blackened and soiled.

"Now don't you cry, honey Miss Lily, and I'll just wash it right out for you, and have it back as clane as a new pin," said the good-natured Hannah. "If I'd known it yesterday, sure I'd a done it then; but niver a wurd did I think of its bein' your work, and it in that state. Och, what a crathur it is, that botherin' little baste!" she added, as she went off with the melancholy looking petticoat in her hand.

"Will she have it washed and dried and ironed in time for me to finish it before the children come, mamma?" asked the sobbing Lily, burying her head in her mother's lap.

"I am afraid not, dear," answered her mother, with a tender, pitying touch upon the thoughtless little head which brought so much trouble upon itself, "so much time has been lost in hunting for your work, and it is now nearly eleven o'clock."

"If I'd only gone to my sewing at first as you advised me, then I'd have found out sooner what that horrid little old hateful puppy had done, and Hannah might have washed the petticoat for me in time," moaned Lily. "I wish Tom never had the puppy."

"I do not think we must blame the puppy, my darling," said her mamma. "He only acted according to his nature; and he found the skirt, you know, where it should not have been."

"Yes," said Lily, "poor little cunning fellow; it wasn't his fault. It was all horrid old me, with my putting off that I never shall cure myself of; no, never, never. It is too mean that I cannot finish that tiresome petticoat this morning."

"Happily, dear, the consequences of your fault are not yet without remedy, and you may still make up for lost time, unless something should happen which we do not foresee; but you have only this one more chance, Lily. Take care that you do not neglect it, or be tempted to procrastinate again."

X.

SATURDAY AFTERNOON'S PLAY.

MRS. Norris was right; for although Hannah did her best, she found it impossible to have the petticoat dry enough to iron so that Lily might have some time to sew upon it before her young friends arrived.

As soon as she had at all recovered her spirits, the little girl relieved her mind in some degree by making frequent rushes to the head of the back stairs to see if Hannah were coming with the petticoat; and once she persuaded her mother to let her go to the laundry that she might "be encouraged by seeing how much Hannah had done."

But she did not receive much encouragement from the sight of the still dripping garment, which Hannah had hung before the fire that it might dry the more quickly. Hannah took a cheerful view of the subject, saying she would have it ready very soon, and there was "lots of time afore Tuesday mornin'." But Lily was at last learning the folly of believing in "lots of time" to come; and she shook her head in a melancholy manner, and bade Hannah "take a lesson of her misfortunes, and never procrastinate."

She returned to the nursery in a very low state of mind, when Nora told her she would dress her at once if she chose, so that if she had any time to spare she might employ it on the skirt when it was dry.

Lily gratefully accepted the offer, but it proved of no use as far as the petticoat was concerned, for she had bade her little friends to "be sure and come by twelve o'clock," and her mamma having seconded the invitation, they had been allowed to do so; and soon after twelve, Maggie, Bessie, Belle, and Mabel arrived, just as Hannah brought up the petticoat, fairly smoking from her hot irons, and five minutes after, the rest of the young party made their appearance.

The clouds passed from Lily's face and mind at the sight of all these "sunbeams," and, consoling herself with the recollection that after all she still had Monday afternoon, she was presently as merry and full of spirits as usual.

Happily not one of the other children thought of asking her if the petticoat were finished, so that she was spared the mortification of confessing that it was not.

It was proposed that they should all amuse themselves downstairs until the early dinner, which had been ordered for them at one o'clock; after which they would go to the grand play-room in the attic, Maggie having provided herself with some fresh proverbs and charades, which they were to play.

68

"Harry and Fred are coming over this afternoon, and we want to make a ship in the lumber-room. You won't mind, will you?" asked Tom, who was taking his lunch at the little girls' dinner.

Doubtful looks were exchanged between some of them. Maggie's looks were not at all doubtful; her face was one of blank dismay at the proposal. Playing charades and proverbs was all very well when there were only those of her own age to look on; doing it before these big boys was quite another thing.

"Not if you don't like it, Maggie," said Tom, noticing her annoyance; "but we wouldn't disturb you, and anyhow I am sure you need not mind having us see you. We'll be busy at the carpenter's bench and tool-chest, and you need not heed us if we do see."

"I'm — I'm afraid you'll — you'll laugh at us," hesitated Maggie, coloring.

"If we laugh, it will be with you, not at you," said Tom. "But never mind; if you don't like it, we'll keep out of your way."

Then Maggie felt self-reproached, and, like the generous little girl she was, determined that her bashfulness should not get the upper hand of her readiness to oblige.

"I don't mind it so very much," she said; "at least I'll try not to, and you can come if the others say so. I suppose you won't take notice of us if you are building a ship, would you, Tom?" she added wistfully.

"No one shall disturb or trouble you in any way, you may believe that," said Tom; and Maggie knew that he would keep his word, and so declared her willingness that the boys should share the privileges of the lumber-room.

Away to the attic scampered the seven pairs of little feet the moment dinner was over; and Nora, following, opened the trunks for them, then left them to their own devices. That is to say, she brought her sewing, and went to sit in one of the rooms which opened out of the great gallery, where she might be within call if the children needed her, and at hand to keep them from mischief. That she provided for her own amusement by leaving the door so that she could see and hear, none of them, not even shy Maggie, noticed or cared.

Maggie of course was always chief spirit and prime manager of these entertainments; and she now divided the party, taking Belle and Nellie with herself as performers in the first charade, and assigning the part of spectators to Bessie, Lily, Carrie, and Mabel.

The audience speedily accommodated themselves and their children — that is their dolls — with seats upon the top of the bins, scrambling thereto by the help of chairs, and amusing themselves with lively conversation while waiting.

Maggie and Nellie brought forth from the store-room a small table and three chairs, which were suitably placed; Sir Percy was brought from his place of repose and laid upon the floor beside them; after which the young ladies retired again into privacy.

"The charade has begun, and Sir Percy is a great big dog this time," said Maggie, suddenly popping out her head once more, and then withdrawing it.

After some moments she reappeared, this time gorgeously arrayed in a flowing train, formed of an old red table-cloth, bordered with gold, a wreath of artificial flowers on her head, ribbons of all colors pinned and tied about her, and an enormous fan in her hand, with which she fanned herself affectedly, mincing and prinking as she walked to a chair, where she seated herself, taking good care to keep her face turned from Sir Percy, whom she pretended not to observe. The audience were spell-bound with interest and the wish to guess the word.

"Tell your mistress—er—that er—Madam Jones—er—is here—er," drawled the lady, addressing an imaginary servant, closing her eyes as if quite exhausted, and putting on all the airs and graces conceivable.

Presently entered the hostess, attired with similar magnificence, but with rather a bluff and off-hand manner, which contrasted very strikingly with that of her visitor. Meanwhile, from behind the door of the store-room came a piteous mewing, which soon attracted the attention of the second lady, who peered about her in great surprise, and exclaimed,—

"That must be a cat mewing, and I never allow a cat in my house, never!"

"Oh—er," drawled Mrs. Jones, "it is only my sweet pussy, my lovely pet, my only donly pet; such a dear pet, oh, such! Wouldn't you like to see her, Mrs. Smith?"

"No, oh, no!" cries Mrs. Smith, lifting up her hands in horror; "I hate cats, and so does my lovely pet, Bombastes Furioso. Here, Bomby, Bomby, Bomby, come and speak to Mrs. Jones, my darling pet."

Upon which Mrs. Jones affected to see for the first time the great dog Bombastes Furioso, and to be filled with alarm at the sight.

"Don't call him, pr-r-r-ay, don't!" she cried. "Is it possible that you like canine dogs, Mrs. Smith? How can you have such a pet? Here, kitty, kitty, kitty!"

Hereupon entered Belle on all fours, covered with a white flossy mat which had been brought up from the hall for the purpose, and ran mewing about her mistress.

"I'd rather like canine dogs than canine cats," wrathfully cries Mrs. Smith; "and, ma'am, I tell you I won't have cats in my house! S'cat, s'cat, s'cat!"

"Ma'am," cries Mrs. Jones, indignantly, "if you turn out my pet, you turn out me, and I'll never visit you again, ma'am, nor be acquainted with you any more. I cut you, ma'am, I cut you!"

"And I cut you, ma'am. Bringing cats in my house, indeed! Here, Bombastes Furioso, s-s-s-s!" and the indignant and inhospitable Mrs. Smith tried to urge her dog to seize Mrs. Jones' kitty. Bombastes, however, being a dog of a lazy turn of mind, contented himself with deep, hoarse growls whenever Mrs. Jones was speaking. He was silent when it was necessary for his mistress to speak; and Mrs. Smith found herself obliged to drag her lumbering pet onwards by his two remaining hoofs—I beg his pardon, I should have said paws.

This was the sole objection to the accommodating Sir Percy, that he was so unwieldy and cumbersome to move when circumstances required that he should do so. This being the case, Mrs. Jones, whose airs and graces were all put to flight by this attack upon her, had time to scuttle off with her pet before Bombastes Furioso had advanced more than a step or two.

This was greeted with shouts of laughter, in which the performers themselves joined as they disappeared; and after the applause had subsided, the four heads on the top of the bins set themselves to guess the word.

"I think it's affected lady," said Carrie.

"I don't. I think it is cat or dog," said Lily. "You know this is only the first syllable, Carrie, so it couldn't be affected lady."

"Oh, to be sure," said Carrie. "Bessie, what do you think it is?"

"I think it is pet," said Bessie. "Did you not hear how often they said 'pet'? 'Pet' dog and 'pet' cat?"

"Yes, so they did," said Lily. "Bessie, you are right. Oh, isn't it fun?"

The performers were not long in making their preparations for the next syllable; and the only change in the outward arrangements was that various bottles, a saw, some chisels, awls, and other tools were brought out, and placed upon the table.

"These are doctors' instruments," Maggie explained before retiring.

Presently she reappeared, buttoned up in an overcoat which reached to her feet, a man's hat coming down over her eyes, a cane in her hand, and bustled round among the bottles. From this occupation the doctor was roused by a knock at the door, and there entered two other overcoated figures, limping and groaning in a distressful manner.

"We've been in a railroad accident, and all our bones are broken, doctor," piped one of the sufferers.

The unfeeling surgeon hustled them each into a chair, and with great roughness proceeded to wrap and bandage, tying a great many knots with much unnecessary vigor, accompanied with shrieks and groans from his patients.

"Ow — ow — ow, doctor," cried one of them, as the doctor pulled hard upon a knot in the handkerchief he was tying on a broken arm, "you do hurt more than any doctor I ever knew. You tie so hard."

"Well," growled the doctor, "when you come to me with two broken arms, and two broken legs, and a broken back, and your eyes put out, and your head smashed up, do you expect to be mended without being hurt? Here, let me tie your head."

The patients, being well tied up, at last departed, followed by the doctor; and the audience unanimously agreed that tie was the second syllable.

"Pet — tie," said Bessie. "I just b'lieve it's petticoat."

"So it is," said Carrie; while Lily, recalled to the recollection of her unfortunate petticoat, was struck dumb by what she considered a remarkable coincidence.

The performance of the third syllable was not quite as interesting as the other two had been, the coats which had been worn by the doctor and his patients being brought out and beaten with sticks with a great bustle and fuss, but without a single spoken word. After this it scarcely needed the performance of the whole word to establish the fact that it was petticoat; but, the chairs and table being removed, it was gone through with by three young ladies, very much dressed, taking a walk on a muddy day, and greatly disturbed for the fate of their petticoats, as they splashed and waded through imaginary pools and puddles.

"Petticoat! Petticoat! Petticoat!" resounded from the top of the bins, accompanied by violent clapping and stamping, and other tokens of the pleasure which had been afforded by the representation.

And now the audience came down from their perch, and resigned it to the late performers, with whom they were to change parts; at least, Belle and Nellie were to do so, for Maggie was, as I have said, the moving spirit, and all the others played under her orders. She was the most ingenious in choosing and arranging the words, and it was believed that no charade went off well unless she took part in it.

This arrangement only left two spectators, it is true; but Maggie said she needed all the others, and no objection was made.

The chairs and table were now brought back to their old places. After the necessary dressing up had been done, Bessie appeared with a handkerchief tied over her sunny curls, a white apron coming down to her feet, and followed by Carrie as a servant, bearing dishes. These — a doll's dinner set — were arranged upon the table with much noise and rattle, the little landlady bustling about, and calling upon her maid to make haste.

"For I keep a very good inn, servant," she said; "but when some people come to inns, they make a great fuss, and give a great deal of trouble; and I heard of a gentleman who is coming to my inn, and he is very cross, and a great scolder, so I don't want to give him any reason to complain, and we must have every thing very nice in my inn."

"Yes, ma'am, we'll have the inn very fine for him," answered the maid.

The fears of the landlady were not unfounded, as it proved; for presently appeared Sir Percy in the character of a cross old gentleman, supported and dragged along with much difficulty by his wife and daughters. He was attired in a man's hat and great-coat, the sleeves of the latter coming down some distance below his — h'm — hands; but this was a convenience, as they could be flapped about in wild gesticulation, as he stormed and scolded at the inconveniences of the inn. A more ill-tempered old gentleman was never seen; and a hard time did his attendants have of it. He laid about him in the most ferocious manner, and was not to be pacified by all the attentions that were lavished upon him; until the little landlady declared that "if that old gentleman was going to stay a great while in her inn, she would not keep an inn any longer."

"Inn, inn," was called, not only from the bins, but also from the other side of the room, as the old man was at last carried away, still growling, and wildly slapping the air with his coat-cuffs.

The children turned, and Sir Percy tumbled heavily to the floor, as Maggie loosened her hold of him, struck dumb by the sight of three pairs of eyes peering above the side of the staircase.

"Now, that's too bad," cried Lily. "You boys can just go 'way. You'll laugh at us."

"Indeed, we won't," said Tom. "We came up just a few moments ago, and we thought we wouldn't interrupt you by passing through, but wait until you had finished, and that was capitally done. But I'm afraid you'll hurt yourselves with Sir Percy. He is too heavy for you to lug about, and Maggie's toes barely escaped just now."

"O Tom!" said Lily; "why, half the fun would be spoiled if we didn't have Sir Percy."

"Well, be careful then," said Tom, as he passed on with Harry into the store-room.

But Fred lingered.

"I say, Midge," he said, "let a fellow stay and see the rest of your charade, will you? It's jolly."

Maggie looked blank, but all she said was, "O Fred!"

"No, you can't," said Lily, unmindful of the duties of hospitality in her own attic; "you just can't, 'cause you'll laugh, and make fun of us."

"Now come on, Fred, and let them alone," called Tom from within the room. "I promised them they should not be teased if we came up here."

"I'm not going to tease them," said Fred. "I want to see the charade, really and truly. The little chaps do it first-rate, and I like it. Let me stay, girls."

Maggie and Bessie, especially the latter, had strong objections to being called "chaps," but Fred never could remember that. However, they passed it by; and Fred won a rather reluctant consent to his remaining as a spectator. He was put upon his good behavior, and with a run and a jump speedily landed himself beside Belle and Carrie, where he kept his word, and conducted himself as a well-behaved spectator should do.

The next syllable presented a lady writing, her maid sewing. In rushes a gardener, tree in hand, represented by a large feather dust-brush; and with much Irish brogue and great excitement, accuses the lady's son of cutting down a young peach-tree. Son denies, and is believed by his mother, who sternly tells the gardener that her son has never told a lie, and whatever he says is "true, true, true."

Gardener declares that "indade, an' he is thrue; an' if the missis will but make Master George Washington hould up the hand that's behint him, she'll see the hatchet he did it with."

Mother demands the hatchet, son rebels, still keeping his hand behind him, but mother, chasing round and round, presently discovers it; whereupon she clasps her hands frantically, cries she thought he was true, falls fainting to the ground, and is carried off by son, gardener, and maid.

This new version of an old and familiar story was received with tremendous applause, to which Fred's boots added not a little.

Next appeared Sir Percy once more, this time without any outward adornments. He was laid upon the floor, and in his mouth was thrust a pointed stick, bearing a paper, on which was written in Maggie's largest, roundest hand, these words: —

"This is a disagreeable smelling dead cat."

About and around the dead cat walked five young ladies, uttering exclamations of disgust, wondering where the smell could come from, but strangely blind to the offensive animal which lay before them.

"Ow! how horrid!" cried one.

"Ugh! disgusting!" exclaimed another.

"What an awful smell!" said the third.

"Ugh! it's that dead cat!" said the fourth. "Let's shun it, let's shun it!"

And with loud cries of "Shun it, shun it," the five young ladies scamper into the store-room, from which the sound of smothered laughter had now and then mingled with the public applause without.

It was not difficult now to guess the word; nevertheless the whole charade must be played out before it was even hinted at to the performers.

"In-tru-sion," was carried out by two of the aforesaid young ladies, who rang violently at a front-door bell, and were denied admittance by a dainty, little sunny-haired maid, who declared that her mistress was very much engaged.

The visitors persisted in their desire to see her, and forced their way in, to be fiercely attacked by the indignant lady of the mansion, who was engaged with her lover, Sir Percy, and who sternly demanded, "Whence this intrusion?"

"No intrusion at all, ma'am," says one of the visitors.

"Yes, intrusion, ma'am," replies the hostess; and contradiction followed free and fast, until stopped by the shouts of "Intrusion! Intrusion!" from the reserved seats.

XI

A SAD ACCIDENT.

"THAT'S capital!" exclaimed Fred. "Give us another, Midge, will you?"

Fred had conducted himself with such becoming propriety, and his applause had been so hearty, that Maggie felt not only quite reconciled to his presence, but also ready to indulge him; and she answered, —

"Yes, I have one more, and it is to be instructive as well as amusing, Fred, because it is an historical charade."

"Go ahead!" said Fred, scrambling back into his seat, which he had left to help carry Sir Percy into retirement.

The preparations for the first syllable of the historical charade were very imposing. Two chairs were placed face to face; upon these was mounted the table, turned upside down, with its legs in the air; to one of the legs was tied a large feather dust-brush, — the whole arrangement supposed to represent an oak-tree, as Maggie explained.

Maggie, Nellie, Lily, and Belle were the performers on this occasion; and in due time they all entered, escorting Sir Percy, now in the character of King Charles, in full kingly costume, the red table-cloth doing duty for his robes, and a crown, a "real crown" of tinsel paper adorning his majesty's brows. He was held with some difficulty upon his horse, — another chair turned down for the purpose, — and again Tom's warning voice came from the store-room.

"You'd better look out with that old hobby. You'll hurt yourselves some time, lugging him about that fashion."

But the suggestion was treated with disdain.

An old hobby indeed! King Charles an "old hobby"!

The horse — that is, the chair horse — paused beneath the tree, and then, relieved of his burden, galloped off, led by Belle; while the other three prepared to hoist his cumbersome majesty into the tree, he not being agile enough to perform that office for himself.

Maggie had proposed that two of the children should be his enemies in pursuit; but no one was willing to take that character. Staunch little royalists they were, every one, and not to be reckoned among the persecutors of the unfortunate king. So this little diversion from the true historical facts had been permitted to suit the occasion, all the more readily as it was feared that it would take the united strength of the whole four to raise him to the necessary height. Still Maggie had not been quite satisfied with such a very great departure from reality; and, hearing the difficulty as they worked at the carpenter's bench, Tom and Harry had good-naturedly offered to take upon themselves the obnoxious part of the king's enemies, and as soon as he was safely hidden in the tree to rush forth in search of him, and feign total unconsciousness as they passed beneath his place of shelter.

This being settled, and Belle, having disposed of her horse, and returned to give a hand to the lifting process, the royal fugitive was, by the united exertions of his four devoted adherents, raised to his hiding-place. But he proved too heavy for the slight construction; and feather duster, chair, and table toppled over together, carrying King Charles with them.

Maggie and Lily held fast, one on either side, but the other two had left their hold. Fred, seeing the danger, sprang like a shot from his seat, and his hand but just touched the old hobby-horse as it rolled over, not soon enough to prevent its fall, but in time to turn the heavy thing a little aside. It fell, carrying Lily back with it; and the two came together to the floor, jarring the whole house. Tom and Harry rushed out, not, alas! in the play in which they had offered to join, but in sad and alarmed earnest; and Nora flew from her work.

Tom had Lily in his arms in an instant, but the poor little girl was a sorry sight. Sir Percy's head had struck against hers as they fell together, and blood was already streaming from an ugly wound just above her temple. But for Fred's timely touch, which turned the weight of the hobby-horse a little to one side, the child's head must have been crushed, and she killed.

Oh, was not Maggie thankful that she had allowed her good-nature to triumph over her fear of being laughed at, and had consented to let Fred join in their fun!

Ah! the fun and frolic were changed now,—changed to distress and alarm. Lily lay half stunned, gasping and death-like, while the cries and shrieks of the other children rang through the house, and speedily brought her mother to the spot.

It was indeed a sad ending to the merry afternoon, and for a few moments the children could scarcely believe that Lily was not killed, or at least dying, so white and quiet did she lie. Never did piteous cry carry more relief to a mother's heart than that which at last broke from the pale, trembling lips; for Mrs. Norris too had feared that her darling was dangerously, if not fatally injured. It must have been so indeed but for the care of the kind Father who had watched over her, and sent Fred's timely help to turn aside a portion of the threatening danger.

"Go for the doctor," said Mrs. Norris.

But Fred, with a thoughtfulness which he sometimes showed, had already asked Tom if he should not do this, and had started off with his direction.

The grass never grew beneath Fred's nimble feet at any time; and now, when he believed there was need for speed, he almost flew over the ground, and, happily finding the doctor at home, brought him back with him at once.

Lily had been carried downstairs and laid upon her little bed, where her mother was doing for her all that she could, though that was not much, until the doctor came.

A group of frightened and distressed little faces met the good old physician's eye as he passed through the hall. He spoke a few cheering words as he went by, but as he did not yet know how much Lily was hurt, he did not put much heart into his young hearers. Still it was a comfort to know that he had come, and it always did one good to see Dr. Banks' kind, helpful face.

Before the doctor arrived, Lily had opened her eyes, and smiled at her mother with a bewildered look; but when she saw the blood which was streaming from the wound in her head, she was frightened, and began to cry again.

But the dear old doctor soon quieted her fears, and those of her anxious mother; and the good news presently spread through the house that he did not think her dangerously hurt. There was a deep, ugly cut on her head just above the temple, it was true, and her eye was already swelling and blackening; but he had no fears that her injuries were serious, and with some care and quiet she would soon be well again.

But Lily had had a very merciful escape, and Maggie could not be sufficiently glad and thankful that she had been kind and obliging, and allowed Fred "to come to the charades," when she heard every one saying that but for the thrust from his hand which had turned aside the weight of the old hobby-horse, the heavy thing must have crushed the dear little head of her young playmate.

"It was quite a mountain of mercy out of a mole-hill of kindness," quaintly said dear Maggie, as she wiped from her eyes the tears of joy and gratitude.

Hearing that Lily must be kept quiet, the thoughtful Harry carried away his sisters, and all the other little visitors, as soon as they were assured that there was no cause for alarm, and saw them all safely to their separate homes.

Lily lay patient and gentle under the doctor's handling, as he felt the poor little bruised head, and tenderly cut away the hair from the wound, and bound it up; but every now and then she put up her hand, with a piteous, anxious expression, to the eye which was swelling and closing so fast.

"Does it pain you so, darling?" her mother would ask.

"Not so very much, mamma," she would answer, "but" — and here her words always came to an end.

But when the doctor was through, and the aching head laid carefully on a soft pillow, the trouble that was weighing on her mind broke forth.

"Doctor," she asked wistfully, "is my eye going out?"

"Going out? No, indeed," answered the doctor, cheerily. "I rather think it is going in, my Lily-bud. It is shutting up pretty tight now, it is true; but we'll take the swelling down in a day or two, and it will soon be as useful and bright as ever."

"By Monday, Doctor?" questioned Lily, anxiously.

"Ho, no, indeed, my little woman! You will not have much use of this peeper for a week or ten days to come. Even if you could see out of it, you must keep quite quiet, lie here on the bed or on the sofa, and be petted and nursed for a few days, or this little head may give you some trouble."

Lily looked as if something was giving her a good deal of trouble now; for as the doctor spoke, her face grew longer and longer, and now she burst into tears again, as she sobbed out, —

"My petticoat! O mamma, my orphan petticoat!"

"Hallo!" said the doctor, "what is that, I should like to know? I have heard of a good many kinds of petticoats, but I never heard of an orphan petticoat before. But this will not do, my child. You must lie down and keep quiet."

"Do not trouble yourself about the petticoat now, darling," said her mother, gently laying her back upon the pillow, from which she had started up in her distress, "I will arrange that."

"But, mamma," said Lily, piteously, "you know you said—you said that you could not let Nora finish it for me, and—and—oh, dear!—you couldn't break your word, you know, and my orphan child won't have any petticoat, and it was all my old Pro, and so what can I do? Oh, if I only didn't have Pro! I b'lieve he's my worst enemy."

"What is all this about petticoats and pro's, Mrs. Norris?" said the doctor. "Put her mind at rest if you can, or we shall be having headache and fever."

"Lily, darling," said her mother, "you must set your mind at rest about the petticoat. You certainly cannot finish it now; but I shall not let the little orphan suffer. By and by I will see what is best to do, but now you must talk and think no more about it. Mamma will arrange it all for you, and you will make yourself worse if you fret."

"Dear mamma," said Lily, "I should think you would want to arrange not to have such a bothering little thing as me for your own little girl; only I don't s'pose you do. I b'lieve mammas generally don't."

"Hush, hush, my darling," said her mother, whose own heart was swelling with gratitude that a Higher Hand had "arranged" that her dear "little bothering thing," as

Lily called herself, was not to be taken from her, but that she was still spared to be the joy of all who loved her, the "sunbeam" of the home that would have seemed so dark without her.

Lily obeyed the soothing touch of her mother's hand, and, confident that she would find some way to help her out of her trouble, said no more of the unfinished task. But it was upon her mind for all that, as was proved when the evening wore away, and the fever and light-headedness the doctor had feared came on. A very slight illness was enough to make Lily light-headed, and the blow she had received was by no means a slight one. So it was not strange that it should have that effect. And she talked pretty wildly about petticoats and puppies, work-boxes and rocking-horses, and had many bitter words for her enemy Pro; and all her mother could say would not soothe her.

But at last she grew more quiet, and the poor little bruised head ceased to wander, and she fell asleep; and when she awoke in the morning, her mind was as bright and clear as ever.

But her face was sadly disfigured, and one eye was quite closed up, so that it was plainly to be seen that Lily would not have much use of it for some days to come. All this would pass away in time, however; swelling and discoloration would disappear by and by; and, happily, the cut upon her head came where the scar would be hidden by her hair.

Somewhat to Mrs. Norris' surprise, Lily said no word of the petticoat all the next day; but she was very glad that it was so, and took pains to avoid any thing that might turn her thoughts that way. Lily did think of it, however, although she said nothing; and she could not but wonder now and then how her mother would contrive to help her without breaking her word. But she felt languid and ill, and it was a trouble to talk, so she let it go for the present, believing as usual that it would come right somehow.

But on Monday morning, when Nora was dressing her, the nurse said,—

"Miss Lily, darling, I am just going to ask your mamma to let me finish your petticoat for you. I think she'll excuse you this once, since you cannot do it for yourself."

"No," said Lily earnestly, "you must not ask mamma, Nora, 'cause it would only give her the uncomfortableness of saying no. She told me she would not let the little orphan suffer for my fault, and she will find a way to make it right, though I don't know what it is, and I am too ashamed to ask her. But you know she said very surely and pos-i-tive-ly, Nora, that she would not let you finish it, if it was not done through my putting off; and that was the reason it was not done on Saturday morning, as it ought to have been. I know I cannot do it now myself, but I could have done it before; and mamma can not break her word."

Lily concluded with a sigh, for she really did not know what plan her mother could have for helping her, and she was very anxious, though, as she said, too much ashamed to ask any more.

But it so happened that Mrs. Norris overheard this conversation, and she was thankful to find how strong in her Lily was that sense of truth which would not allow her to believe for one moment that mamma could go back from her word under any circumstances. It was rather remarkable that with all her heedlessness and volatile spirits, Lily was so strictly truthful and upright, for they never betrayed her into an equivocation, as carelessness and want of thought are too apt to do.

The morning was not far gone before Lily's mind was set at rest on the subject of her petticoat, for her mamma came to sit beside her, and brought her work with her.

And what was her work?

Lily noticed it in a moment; a petticoat for a child,—not of such muslin as her own skirts, but coarser and stronger, just such as her "orphan petticoat" was made of.

"Mamma?" she said, with her eyes fixed upon the strips of muslin in her mother's hand.

"Yes, dear," said her mother, "you know I said the little orphan must not suffer through you, and I told you Nora could not finish your petticoat, and send it as your work, if you did not do it yourself; so I shall make this one, and send it to Miss Ashton in the place of the other."

"And tell Miss Ashton, mamma?"

"Well, yes, dear, I must. Do you not think so?"

"Yes, mamma, and I s'pose the girls must know. Even if she don't tell them, I think I ought to when I go back to school. They ought not to think I was industrious and good like the rest when I just put off and put off until this sad accident came, and then I really couldn't do it;" and here a great tear rolled down Lily's cheek.

"My darling," said her mother, dropping her work, and bending over to kiss the sorrowful little face, "mamma cannot bear to see you mortified and grieved, but she does want this to be a lesson to you, and to save you from future trouble and loss."

"Yes, mamma, I know," answered Lily, "and it serves me quite right; but it does make me feel very badly to know that all the other children can feel that the little orphans are having some good of their kindness, and they do not have one bit of mine."

Mrs. Norris hesitated before she spoke again. She felt as if she could not bear to have her poor child so hardly punished now when she was suffering, and had just escaped such a great danger. She could not let Nora finish the petticoat, but why not finish it herself, she thought, as well as make another, and send it to Miss Ashton with a message from Lily that she had not done the whole of it herself?

Just then came a knock at the door, and, being bidden to enter, Robert brought a note for Miss Lily, saying the messenger waited for an answer.

"It is Maggie's writing, I think," said Mrs. Norris.

Lily raised herself, and held out her hand.

"You cannot read it for yourself, dear. Shall I do it?" asked her mother.

Lily assented, and, opening the note, Mrs. Norris read as follows:—

"DEAR LILY,—We are so sorry for you, all of us, but we are so very happy you were not killed by Sir Percy Hotspur, who is very nice to play with, but not nice to fall underneath, and we are glad you are not such a victim as that. But, Lily, dear, we do not know, Bessie and I, if you have finished your petticoat for the orphan child. We did not ask you on Saturday because we thought if it was not done you wouldn't like to say so, but we thought perhaps the reason you did not speak about it was because a 'burnt child dreads the fire,' which means people don't like things that bring them into trouble, or to speak about them. So we thought it was quite probable that it was not done, and we know you cannot finish it now, for yesterday we met Dr. Banks when we were coming from church, and he said you could not go to school, or use your poor hurt eye for a good many days. So, dear, if you would let me finish it for you, I would be very glad, and Bessie will too, and you can send it to me by Patrick. And you need not think I will have to do it all in my play-time, for mamma says I can do it in my sewing-lesson to-day, which is half an hour, and if there is any more, I'd just as lieve do it afterwards, and the heart which would not do that is not worthy of a friend, but ought to be like a man we read about the other day who lived in a tub and was cross to everybody. And do you believe, people called him a wise man!!! Which shows they must have been very stupid people in those days to call such an old cross-patch wise, and I'm glad I was never acquainted with him for I would not consider him fit to know.

"So ask your mamma to send me the petticoat if it is not done, that my true friendship may have the pleasure of finishing it. From your esteemed friend,

"MAGGIE STANTON BRADFORD.

"P.S. If a pretty bad button-hole would be any relief to your feelings instead of strings, I would just as lieve make one, but it don't look very nice."

To have seen Lily's eyes—or rather her eye, for you know there was only one to be seen—as her mother finished reading this letter to her! to have seen the pleading of her poor little face!

"Well, dear," said her mother, smiling back in answer to the unspoken question that was written in every line of her Lily's countenance. "Well, dear, shall we accept Maggie's offer?"

"Oh, mamma! if you think I might," cried Lily.

"Yes," said her mother, "since dear Maggie is so good as to offer, and give up her time to you, perhaps I will let you accept. But, my darling, I do not want you to forget that here again the consequences of your habit of procrastinating are falling on another. Maggie is doing the work which should have been done by you, and although, I am sure she does it willingly, and with all her heart, dear little friend that she is, still you must own that it is hard she should have her own share, and part of yours too."

"Yes, mamma," answered Lily, penitently, "and I know I don't deserve to have any of the work I have done go to the orphan that has no father or mother, and I am very thankful to darling Maggie. And, mamma, I think I ought to ask you to write a note to Miss Ashton, and let her tell the other children that I did not do the whole of the petticoat, or it would not be quite fair. 'Specially, mamma, 'cause some of them said I wouldn't have my petticoat done, and I scorned what they said, and was very sure of myself. So it would be more true, I think, to tell them how it was."

"Yes, darling," said her mother, glad that her little girl was so truthful, and unwilling to take any credit that was not rightly her own; and then she kissed her, and, bringing the unfortunate petticoat, rolled it up, and sent it away to the dear little sunbeam who was so ready to shed light and comfort wherever she had the power to do so.

XII

LILY'S NEW RESOLVE.

THERE was a good deal of bustle and excitement, as you may imagine, on Tuesday morning, when Miss Ashton's little scholars came, each with her respective parcel.

Poor Lily of course was not there; it would be many a day yet before she was able to come to school, but all the others were in their places, and very anxious for the lessons to be over. Nor were Maggie and Bessie there during school-hours; but they were to come afterwards, and bring the little garments they had made.

"Let's see who finished her work first," said Gracie. "Dora, when did you finish yours?"

"Saturday morning," answered Dora.

"Pooh!" said Gracie, "how long you were. Nellie, when was yours done?"

"Last night," answered Nellie; "and I was very glad I had not taken a petticoat, for I could not have finished it."

Gracie only looked her contempt, but she did that so plainly that it might have placed her in the ranks of the anti-politers quite as readily as rude and scornful words could have done. Nellie felt it, colored, and looked hurt.

"Belle, when did you finish yours?"

"I perfer not to tell you," answered Belle, with magnificence.

"Why?" asked Gracie.

"If your guilty conscience don't tell you, it's no use for me to speak about it," replied Belle, with well-deserved severity, supposed to be kept within the bounds of courteousness.

Gracie gave her head a little toss, as much as to say that Belle's opinion was quite beneath her notice; but that her "guilty conscience" did accuse her was to be seen from the fact that she questioned no more of her classmates, but said conceitedly, —

"I finished my petticoat the very Saturday after I took it;" and then looked about her for the applause which no one had the mind to offer.

It was strange that the frequency of the disappointments of this nature which she received did not teach Gracie that those who sought the most eagerly for food for their own vanity were not the most apt to receive it; but her insatiable self-conceit needed some severe teaching before it would lose its hold of her, and such slight blows as these were without much effect on the still increasing evil.

"I am sure I could easily have made two if I had chosen," continued Gracie. "It is nothing so very great to make a petticoat in a week."

"I don't know," said Nellie, who seldom bore malice, "I think it is pretty well for little girls to make one in two weeks. I am slow, I know, but as Lily said,—poor dear Lily,—I am a steady tortoise after all, and have done my task in time."

"Is Lily's petticoat finished?" asked Mabel. "Does any one know?"

No, no one knew; but more than one thought it quite likely that Lily would be behindhand. They knew her ways well. But, before they had time for much more conversation on the subject, Miss Ashton came in, and the business of the day began.

Twelve o'clock came, bringing with it Maggie and Bessie, who also brought each the little garment she had completed; and, school being at an end, the children gathered about Miss Ashton to have her verdict on their work.

Belle's bag was the first to be examined, and Miss Ashton pronounced it very well done for a little girl who was but just learning to sew. There were some long and crooked stitches, it is true; but they were tight and close, and showed that she had taken great pains. So did Bessie's; and Mabel's also was considered a success. Carrie Ransom's did not show quite as much care, but it would pass. So much for the bags made by the four lesser children; and now Miss Ashton turned to the petticoats.

"I have here a note from Lily," she said, "which I shall read first. She sent it to me this morning, with her work, and a request that I would tell you what it contained."

"Oh," said Gracie, "I suppose she has not finished her petticoat. She never does things when she ought to, and she is always behindhand. I finished my petticoat on the first Saturday, Miss Ashton."

Now, would you not have thought that Gracie disliked Lily, and was glad to have the chance of showing up her faults? But it was not really so; for if you had asked Gracie, she would have told you that she was fond of Lily, and thought her on the whole a very good little girl. But Gracie's habit of comparing herself with others to their disadvantage gave her, not only the appearance of great conceit, but also of constant fault-finding with her companions.

Miss Ashton took no notice of her speech, but opened the envelope, and took out the note, which Mrs. Norris had written at Lily's dictation.

"Miss Ashton," repeated Gracie, "I finished my petticoat Saturday before last, every stitch of it."

"Very well," said Miss Ashton, coolly, and without farther attention, read aloud:—

"DEAR MISS ASHTON,—I think I ought to tell you that I did not do all my petticoat myself, and it was not all because of my hurting myself, but because I did not do it in good time, but put off until I had left a good task for the last day, when my eye was so hurt I could not sew. But dear Maggie had her's all done, and so she had time for a kindness, and she finished mine; but I thought I ought to do myself the mortification of telling you about it, for fear you and the other children should give me praise I did not deserve.

"And now I am very sorry I was so sure of myself to be so certain I would not fall into my bad habit again, which I find is not cured, as I said it was; but I have to try very hard yet. And I know the other children will think I thought myself very great, and I am ashamed of it, and of my procrastination too, dear Miss Ashton, which you told me would give me great trouble, and mamma too, and I see it. So please excuse me, and my eye and my head are better, thank you; but the doctor says I cannot use my eye for a good many days, and my head aches some yet.

"Please give my love to all the children, and tell them to come and see me.

"From your affectionate little scholar,

"LILY NORRIS."

If Lily's schoolmates did imagine that she thought herself "great," not one of them said so; and the reading of her letter was followed by many expressions of affection and sympathy, mingled with admiration for her straightforward honesty, which would not let her receive credit which was not her due.

However, when Miss Ashton unfolded the petticoat sent by Lily, and examined the sewing, it was found that, wanting though she might have been in punctuality and industry, Lily certainly deserved praise for the manner in which her work was done. It was extremely neat and even for such a little girl; and both her own share, and that completed by Maggie Bradford received much approbation from Miss Ashton.

Maggie's petticoat merited a like meed of compliment, and Nellie Ransom's apron, which came next, was pronounced remarkably well done.

"Why, Nellie, my dear," said Miss Ashton, looking with surprise at the neatly laid gathers, even hems, and regular stitches, "is it possible that you did this all yourself?"

"Yes, ma'am," answered steady, painstaking Nellie, who, although she was perhaps less quick than any of her schoolmates, was seldom or never behind the rest, for the reason that she was so industrious and earnest,—"yes, ma'am. An apron was not very much for me to do, but I wanted to be sure and have it nicely done."

"And, indeed, you have," said Miss Ashton, still examining the apron with pleasure. "I must give you the credit, Nellie, of saying that I never saw a piece of work better done by any child of your age. I do not know that I I would have done it as well myself."

"Mamma takes great pains to teach me to sew nicely," said Nellie, dimpling and flushing with pleasure at her teacher's praise.

"And you must have taken great pains to learn, my dear," said Miss Ashton, laying her hand on that of the modest little girl.

Two or three others received their share of praise, some more, some less, according to their merits, though all were fairly done; and then Miss Ashton came to Gracie's petticoat.

That it gave her far less satisfaction than the rest of the little garments had done, was plainly to be seen by her countenance, as she examined it.

"Why, Gracie, my dear," she said, "is it possible that you can sew no better than this? No, it is not; for I have seen your work before, and know that you can do better if you choose. Why, Gracie, the stitches are not half as neat as those of the very little girls, and this band will not hold at all. It is impossible for me to give in such work as this. See here;" and as she drew the stitches slightly apart, with not half the strain that would come upon them in the wearing, they parted and ripped, showing with what extreme carelessness the work had been done.

I do not think Miss Ashton would have said as much to any other one of her little scholars; but she thought that this mortification and blow to her self-conceit would do Gracie no harm.

"My dear," she continued, "you have not taken time enough to do your work properly. Another time, better less haste and more care, Gracie. I shall have to take out almost the whole of this, and do it over myself, for I should be ashamed that our little orphans should have the example of such work. Your mother was away, I know, so that you could not go to her for help; but could you not ask some other person to show you how it should be done?"

"I should think I might know how to make a petticoat," said Gracie, rather saucily.

"It seems you do not," replied Miss Ashton, gravely. "As I must do this over, you cannot expect that it should be given in as your work, Gracie."

Gracie tossed her head, and looked very angry, muttering, she "did not care," then burst into tears, saying it was "too bad," and "real mean," and she knew "it was just as good as the rest, only Miss Ashton never would think she did any thing fit to be seen," and altogether allowed her temper and wounded vanity so far to get the better of her that Miss Ashton bade her leave the room.

I am glad to say, however, that a few moments' solitude and reflection in the cloak-room brought her to her right senses; and before she went home, she returned to her teacher, and begged her pardon for the temper and disrespect she had shown.

"But my work was finished long before any of the other children's, Miss Ashton," she said once more, after the lady had assured her she was forgiven, giving her at the same time a gentle, and, alas! too oft-repeated warning against the hold her besetting sin was gaining on her temper and character.

Miss Ashton shook her head.

"But it is all thrown away, and worse than thrown away, Gracie," she said, "for it will need more time for me to take it to pieces and do it over again than it would have taken to make it myself at once. I can give you no credit, my child, for striving to outstrip your schoolmates, merely that you might have the pleasure of saying that you had done so. You are severe with Lily for her want of punctuality and promptness; but too great haste, especially when it springs from a bad motive, is perhaps as bad. And, Gracie, Lily sees and acknowledges her fault, while you will not."

Gracie hung her head, but she was none the more convinced; and, in spite of her confession, went home, thinking herself hardly used, and Miss Ashton very unjust.

With the exception of Gracie, there was not one of the little work-women whose sewing was not at least passable, and her garment tolerably well made; and they were dismissed, well satisfied with the praise they received, and the knowledge that their own self-denial and effort had helped those who were in need.

Mrs. Norris had begged that Maggie and Bessie would come and see Lily that afternoon, as she was now well enough to receive them, and tell her all that had taken place in the morning; and accordingly they presented themselves in Lily's room, bringing with them their dolls.

"My dollies haven't had their dresses changed since Saturday, before I was hurt," said Lily, at the sight of the last-mentioned young ladies. "Will you dress them for me while you tell me about this morning?"

Dolls and dolls' clothes were brought forth, Lily possessing a multitude of both; and the two little sisters fell to dressing the neglected children of an invalid mamma.

"It wasn't putting off this time," said Lily, apologetically, "for I really did seem to be so tired every time I tried to do any thing, even play, that mamma told me I had better lie still."

"Yes, we know," said Bessie, "and even if it was procrastination, dolls don't really suffer, so I s'pose it's not much harm to put off doing things for them. It don't hurt," she added thoughtfully, as she drew a comb about three inches long through the flowing locks of the waxen Georgianna upon her lap, — "it don't hurt to put off play and pleasure, I believe, but only duties, and things that will do good to others."

"Yes," said Lily, rather ruefully, as if she wished that pleasures and duties might alike fall under the same head, "so I find most people think. The trouble of it, and what makes it so hard is, that when a duty and a pleasure both come at once, it 'most always seems right to take the duty first; and I like pleasure so much better than duty that I expect that's the reason I procrastinate so often."

"I believe that's the case with most people," said Maggie, putting on her wisdom cap to suit the solemnity of the conversation. "I find the human race generally like pleasure better than duty, 'specially if the duty is very disagreeable, and the pleasure is very nice."

"That's the way with me, anyhow," said Lily, with a sigh, as she lay back upon her sofa pillows once more. "And sometimes, even when the duty is not very disagreeable, I feel like putting it off, just because I know I ought to do it, I believe. That petticoat was not so very horrid to do, and yet I let every thing put me away from doing it, till at last you know the consequence."

"Miss Ashton praised your petticoat very much, anyhow," said Maggie. "She said you had done the most of it, and it was all well done."

"She praised Maggie's part too," said Bessie, unwilling that her sister should not receive her full share of credit, "and she said the button-hole was even better than that on Maggie's own petticoat."

"Practice makes perfect, you know," said Maggie. "Miss Ashton said not one piece of work was better made than that petticoat, except Nellie's apron, and that was the best of all. Miss Ashton seemed quite surprised at it, it was so very nice. And I don't mean to tell tales about Gracie, but you would hear about it, I suppose, when you go back to school, so we may as well tell you, 'cause you want to know about every thing."

And between them, first one taking up the tale, and then the other, Lily had soon heard a full and particular account of all the occurrences of the morning.

"And did not any one say hateful things about me when Miss Ashton read my letter, and they knew I had not done what I was so sure I would do?" asked Lily.

"No indeed," said Bessie. "We wouldn't have listened to them if they had wanted to; but then no one would say an unkind thing about you when you were so honest and true, Lily. They were only sorry for you, and didn't seem to think you were naughty one bit."

"But I was," said Lily, "and I'm never going to boast myself again, for I do feel too ashamed when I think how sure I was that I would do so much. I don't believe I ever will cure myself of procrastination, do you?"

"Why, yes," answered Bessie, "if you try enough."

"I'm sure I did try," said Lily, "but it was no use. If I did not forget so easily, I think I would not have so much trouble from procrastination; but, you see, sometimes I leave a thing just for one moment, at least I mean to come back in a moment, and then I never think any thing more about it. That was the way the puppy found my petticoat lying on the floor, and dragged it about till it had to be washed before I could sew on it, and then it was too late."

"I used to be just as careless as that," said Maggie; "and though mamma says I have improved a great deal, and am pretty neat and careful now, yet I find it hard work still, and I have to make a rule for myself not to leave a thing one moment after I know I ought to do it, or else I am almost sure to forget. I don't always keep that rule yet," she added, rather remorsefully, "but it helps me, and makes me better than I used to be."

"Is that what cured you of carelessness? for I don't think you are much careless now," said Lily.

"Yes," said Maggie, slowly, "that—and—and"—here she fell into a sudden fit of bashfulness at her own confession, and Bessie had to help her out of it.

"Partly that, and partly because she asked Jesus to help her," said the little sister. "And He did, 'cause He always does if we really and truly ask Him. Did you ever ask Him to help you, Lily?"

"What, about putting off?" said Lily. "Why, no, I never thought much about it—and—besides—it seems such a queer thing to pray about, and to ask Jesus to help you in. It is not a sin, you know. It does make me sin sometimes," she added, thoughtfully, as she recalled various naughtinesses into which her sad habit had led her. "Oh, if you knew something it had made me do, you would think I was too horrid!" She was thinking of the way in which she had spoken to her mother but a few days since.

"Well, then," said Bessie, tenderly, "isn't that a reason for asking Him? I don't b'lieve Jesus thinks any thing is no matter if it makes us do something that is wrong, and I don't b'lieve He thinks even a bad habit is a little thing, and I'm sure He'll help you if you only ask Him."

"Sometimes when I was praying, I have thought maybe I had better ask Jesus not to let me put off," said Lily, "but I did not think much about it, and it hardly seemed worth while, and I generally thought I could do it some other time."

Lily said these last words in rather a shamefaced manner, as if she were mortified to recollect and confess that she had allowed her failing to come even between her and the Great Helper.

"But you will ask Him now, won't you?" asked Bessie anxiously.

"Yes, I will," said Lily earnestly, and as if she really meant it; and I am glad to say that she kept her resolution, and "put off" no longer asking the help which could not, and would not fail her. And receiving what she sought, as all shall do who seek it in truth, and in the right spirit, and continuing also to strive with the temptation of the moment which bids her postpone the duty before her, our Lily is gaining the victory over the enemy which brought her into so much trouble, and had more than once led her so far astray.